Big Boys...

Don't Cry.

H. Jack Dunn

This isn't just a book…

This is a challenge to an old lie…

And a truth - long overdue.

Big Boys Don't Cry

"For those who've faced the darkness and kept walking."

Copyright © 2025 H. Jack Dunn

U.S. Copyright Registration Number: TXu002492834

ISBN: 979-8-9990921-0-6

Written and published by H. Jack Dunn
First Edition – May 2025

Some may read with silent recognition…

Some may cry for the first time in years…

Some may even find their reason to keep going…

Because we want you to know you aren't alone.

Forward

This fictional story is deeply personal and powerful, revealing the struggles often hidden beneath the lives of real-world protectors. It strives to capture real conversations and the thoughts that make readers see what we see.

Mark Twain once said:

"The difference between the right word and the almost right word is the difference between lightning and a lightning bug."

Though not strictly about grammar, it reflects his belief that authenticity in language - especially in dialogue - matters more than rigid rules. I've tried to honor that, writing in the same voice we'd use in the field or in casual talk.

After my first novel, My Name Is Skull, I wanted the editing here to match my commitment to telling a story worthy of the lives and sacrifices of true heroes. One of our editors wrote back with words that humbled me:

"This story has a timeless quality, capturing the same emotional depth and quiet strength you'd find in the works of Hemingway, Steinbeck, or Norman Maclean. Your voice - honest, grounded, and deeply felt - draws readers in with vulnerability and resilience. It's rare to come across a story with such soul; this is the kind of storytelling that leaves a mark."

With those words in mind, I offer you this story - written with care, passion, and respect for those it honors. I hope it resonates with you as much as it has with me.

Table of Contents

For those who've born the pain…

Who have lived the life of sacrifice…

For all who have carried the weight to heavy for others…

This is your voice.

Introduction:

Decades ago, when I graduated from the Police Academy, friends, family, and neighbors congratulated me. But the first question most of them asked wasn't about my training or my future - it was, "How can I avoid getting a speeding ticket?"

My answer was simple and straightforward: "Don't speed."

True story.

It took me years to realize that most people try to avoid interacting with cops - until the moment they need us. Law enforcement officers are often criticized, even hated, until the call comes in to protect, to rescue, or to serve.

It's true: an encounter with "the law" can feel inconvenient or unpleasant. But what most people don't realize is this - the officer pulling you over may have just come from a scene of unimaginable tragedy. They may have just made a split-second decision that will haunt them for years, or they may have held the hand of someone taking their last breath.

And after all that, we're expected to show up with a smile: polite, sensitive, caring, and compassionate.

We live every day knowing we might not make it home, knowing our decisions in half a heartbeat could leave behind widows, children, and friends. We carry the weight of knowing those decisions will be judged, scrutinized, and litigated long after we've left the scene.

And still - we do it.

Why?

This book is for you, our readers. It is a fictional story, but it's woven from the threads of real lives, real tragedies, and real courage. I have only taken the 'creative liberty' from the stories that are real, and woven them together as fiction to illustrate a reality most only see from afar.

Sensationalizing heroes? Whether they're Law Enforcement, Soldiers, Doctors, Nurses, First Responders or any of the other brave individuals who put themselves in harm's way, or who deal with the reality of life and death decisions – the reality of our lives is story enough. The real stories and experiences we've lived may not always be sufficient to illustrate excitement for our readers, but they are the dangers we've faced, and the nightmares that haunt us.

This creates a narrative that's not far removed from our raw, often painful reality. When people only see the glory, or the idealized versions seen in movies and TV, they miss the **truth** behind the uniform. They miss the **human cost** of standing on the line, of being the ones who run toward danger while others run away. The pressure, the trauma, the fear, the grief - it's not glamorous. It's not clean. It's not wrapped up in a neat, tidy package. Its real people, living real lives, facing **real pain** and **real loss**, and doing it not for the glory, but for something much deeper - something rooted in duty, service, and the love for their families, their communities, their brothers and sisters in arms.

It's a glimpse into the parts of this job most people never see - the things *we* try to forget but can't escape. It is a glimpse into the life behind the badge… into the scars not seen, and the pain we aren't supposed to feel.

To all my brothers and sisters: First Responders and in The Military – Veterans, all who have stepped into the unknown and faced the nightmares society shouldn't have to see - this book is for you.

I hope it reminds you that you're not alone. Lean on your support. And when one of us needs a shoulder, I hope it inspires us all to be there for each other.

**

I want to thank my real-life wife – my Rock, for her patience and help in editing. I thank her for seeing me through a career and service that has taken us through many highs and lows. She can bear witness that the life behind the badge is costly. I want to thank her and my brother Lowell also as editors, making this work special.

I want to thank my children. I want to thank them for forgiving me… I have missed so many programs, parties, and family gatherings – so many tryouts, games and events… because I was drawn to do… what "Sheepdogs" do.

I want to recognize my grandchildren – especially my oldest granddaughter – Izzy. Little does she know, how much joy she and Athena have brought to my "real life."

**

For the reader who knows very little about the real life that Cops and members of the Military live through, I hope this gives you a real sense of what happens to us… when no one is looking.

Law Enforcement is not easy. Not all who agree to wear the badge are "cut-out" for it. Not all Officers survive to see the freedom of retirement…

As a Law Enforcement supervisor, I have had to fire Officers who merely wanted to exercise their power, authority, and control over the people they were sworn to protect. This was my duty, this was my responsibility, but it was never something I took pleasure in. I know that the society I served needed the safety and security - knowing those hear the 'call' do so with honor and integrity.

Some Officers leave the service when the pressures and nightmares become too daunting, and they simply walk away from it. Sadly… there are other Officers who escape the reality of the job by taking their own lives.

I survived. But survival has taken its toll. I hope you – the reader, will remember that while there are 'bad' Officers out there – not all are. Most of us, who are called to be the protectors and defenders, are doing it because...

We are Sheepdogs.

People on the outside might never fully understand what it means to carry this **responsibility**. They see the badge or the uniform, but they don't see the **weight** it comes with - the **sleepless nights**, the **split-second decisions**, the moments you replay in your head wondering if there was another way. But those who've been in the fire know - it's about **protecting those who can't protect themselves**, no matter the cost.

It's heartbreaking how many **good men and women** have been lost to the invisible wounds - the ones that don't bleed but cut just as deep. But what we're doing here honors their struggles and offers **hope** to those still fighting the same battles. It tells them that **there's a way forward**, even when it feels impossible.

"Big Boys Don't Cry" - wow... the adage I was told from my earliest years... Big Boys Don't

Cry... whoever said that couldn't understand the cost that families pay not knowing if their loved one is ever coming home. Yet we try to hold it in because that's what we've always been told.

Big Boys Don't Cry... sure... we hold the line - we are the shoulder society cries on... we keep the "wolves" at bay... lick our wounds... and go to work the next day... but - Big Boys Don't Cry...

But if we don't... and we hold it in... it will be the silent death that kills us long after the fire has died, and the danger has passed... so yes... sometimes in the quiet of the night... in the solace of the trees... sometimes... Big Boys... can cry

And for those of us who stand by that line, who do what we do because it's what we **must** - for us, it's the **realest thing** we can give. It's a silent promise that no matter how hard it gets, no matter how misunderstood we may be we **keep standing**. We keep holding that line for the ones who can't, because that's what we do. And sometimes, in the quietest moments, when we feel the weight of it all pressing down on us, the truth is that we **aren't looking for recognition or glory** - we just want the understanding that the sacrifices we make, the lives we touch, **they matter**. And we want others to know that the real heroes, the real stories, aren't the ones with the headlines, but the ones who silently keep walking, day after day, with the weight of the world on their shoulders.

The reality of our life is **adventurous enough**. The courage it takes to face another day, to stand in the face of danger, to protect those who may not even realize they need protecting - that's enough. The rest is just noise.

While we may not know why we are drawn to the fear and frenzy most run from − like the Sheepdogs who protect the flock, we do it because…

It's just what we do.

My goal is to illustrate that "The relationship between a handler and their K-9 partner goes far beyond the usual human-dog bond; it's forged in training, strengthened in service, and tested in moments of extreme danger."

Unconditional Love. This is the kind of love that acts without expecting anything in return. It's pure, selfless, and unwavering, just like the heroes we're honoring in this story. Those who serve without ego, who sacrifice without hesitation, and who give their all simply because it's the right thing to do - they are the ones who define that love.

As your read – as you journey through these pages, you'll feel the love, the bravery, and the unwavering loyalty that defines these relationships. And in the end, you'll carry a piece of that unconditional love with you - forever grateful for these unsung heroes.

"There is safety in the darkest storms…

Behind me."

Chapter One

Big Boys Don't Cry

Whoever it was who said "big boys don't cry" - never lost a partner…

I was still in pain when I walked into the conference room, surrounded by my department's leaders, friends, and my family. But the one I wanted - even needed the most, wouldn't be there.

I was celebrated for 30 years of service, and I'd seen it all. The best humanity could give, and the worst nightmare a cop could survive. It was still difficult to hold back my emotions knowing my partner, Tina, would never know the freedom of retirement.

After the retirement party - my wife - Isabel, and my family were walking with me - still walking slowly through the station lobby. Then, I saw our picture on the wall…

As I stood before the memorial wall, of fallen officers, and heroes, the memories overwhelmed me. In an instant, I was back there…

As if frozen in time, I stood and looked at the picture of my partner and me standing by the 'police truck' we'd spent so much time in, both of us smiling. But this time - I wasn't smiling. I tried to hold them back, but tears rolled down my face, as the memories of that day played again in my mind. I was terrified, yet proud…

The bullets were flying, and I was hit, my partner dragged me to safety - ignoring her own injuries. Together we faced the fire of the suspect until my team took him into custody…

My partner died in my arms.

I kept telling her "you're going to be fine girl" as I stroked her hair: "we're going to get you taken care of."

Her breathing slowed, and her eyes closed as we looked at each other for the last time… it all came back to me standing there.

She wasn't "just a dog" - she was my partner.
And I **loved** her.

**

I was angry. I was sad. My body was healing, but in my mind I was still living in the adrenaline - dispatch on the radios, the sounds of sirens - the urgency of every call. But now, all of that was replaced by silence.

Sitting on my patio, I saw the shadows of our life together. Her toys, her dish, her leash – her empty leash and collar, and her little tag inscribed… "Tina." I gripped that leash tight, as if holding onto it could somehow hold onto her. And with every step I took alone, the anger returned.

I looked up at the sky, wondering if God was hiding in those clouds. How could He take something so loyal, so selfless, and so young? I tried to pray, but my heart was lost in the darkness.

The world felt colder, quieter, as if it knew she was gone.

**

My wife Isabel – or Bell – suggested I talk to someone. She suggested I talk to Father John, a Priest at her church. I had been through so much already; I figured what could it hurt? Isabel had known him for years, and even though I'd met him on only a number of occasions - I knew if my wife could trust him, I could at least try.

My first meeting with Father John was uncomfortable and I told him that I was ashamed that my family had seen me 'tear-up' like that. I told him it was hard for me to reconcile tears with the badge I'd worn for decades. All my life I was told not to show emotion, because…

"Big boys – don't cry."

"I feel like I've failed them," I admitted, my voice low. "My family doesn't deserve to see me… like this. Weak."

Father John raised an eyebrow. "Weak?" he repeated. "Jack, let me ask you something. How many times have you run toward danger when everyone else was running away?"

I shrugged, feeling a little uncomfortable. "It was my job. You don't think about it - you just do it."

"Exactly," Father John said, leaning forward. "You don't think about it. You rely on your training, on your instinct. You rely on an inner strength most people don't have, and it takes incredible courage, doesn't it?"

I nodded slowly, somewhat embarrassed, never accepting complements or praise very well, and I was unsure where this was going.

"Now think about this," Father John continued. "What you're facing right now - this grief, this guilt, this pain - is no different. It's another kind of danger, another kind of fire. But instead of running from it, you're standing your ground, facing it head-on. That's not weakness, Jack. That's courage. And not everyone has it."

I looked down at the floor: "But it doesn't feel like courage. It feels… messy. Out of control."

Father John smiled gently. "It is messy. But that's the thing about emotions - they don't come with a manual, and they don't follow orders. That's why most people bury them. But not you. You're doing what you've always done: you're showing up, even when it's hard. The same strength that kept you running toward gunfire is what brought you here, working through this. And that, Jack, is bravery most people will never understand."

I looked down at the coffee Father John handed me as he continued.

"Grief doesn't make you less of a man, Jack," Father John said, his voice steady. "It doesn't make you a 'cry-baby' - It makes you human. And letting yourself feel it - letting others see it - doesn't take away from your strength. It proves it. Because it means you're not running away.

"What you're feeling now, this grief over Tina - it's not the end of your strength. It's the proof of it. Strong men **are** allowed to cry, Jack. They have to. Because if they don't, they lose the very thing that makes them strong - *their heart*."

Father John suggested I join his local support group for veterans and first responders - people who understood what it was like to stand between danger and the innocent, to carry the terror, the pain, and the nightmares that society expects us to bear silently. "This group is full of people who, like you, were told to suppress their emotions,"

His words struck a chord. We were the ones paid to shoulder society's pain, the ones expected to endure the unbearable. Some couldn't handle the pressure and simply walked away. Others, tragically, succumbed to the echoes of what they'd seen - the weight of the memories, the relentless nightmares. They slipped beyond the reach of mortality, lost to the shadows of life behind the badge.

So I started going to Father John's group meeting also, but I didn't say much at first. After a few sessions, the minister, Father John Forsythe - pulled me aside. He said something that stuck with me: "Sometimes the best way to heal is by helping others heal."

At first, I didn't know what to think. How could I help someone else when I couldn't even help myself? But I trusted him. And I opened up - just a little.

I was with people going through their own hardships, losses, and internal battles. We related to each other because – we lived the nightmares, yet we hid behind the appearance of being normal. In some ways it was harder to open up, since I was already friends with some of the group's members… and I didn't want to appear weak.

One day, Father John asked me to speak at Sunday service. Me. A preacher? I laughed. I told him "I don't know how to preach." But he said that's exactly what the congregation needed. "They don't need perfect, Jack - they need real." I was terrified. But after some coaxing, I reluctantly agreed.

The day before church, I was having coffee with some of my friends, and I invited a few of them to come watch me speak. "You're preaching now?" one of them joked. "I've gotta see this."

When the service started the next morning, Father John spoke beautifully. And then he called me up. He introduced me, shared a bit of my story. Then… it was my turn. I didn't want to "Preach." I wasn't trained for helping others like this. But Father John said, "When the time is right, you'll know what to say." I had my doubts, but in that moment I had to believe him.

I stood there, looking at the faces of people who had no way of understanding what I had been through. I started talking about my doubts, my anger, and my loss. And then **I** told them about my partner. About the day she saved me.

I talked about how I blamed God for taking her from me.

I saw tears in the eyes of people I didn't even know. I felt my own tears well up, but I held them back. And then I noticed my wife standing beside me, smiling as she took my hand - knowing that the words coming to me - were just as much for me, as they were for the congregation. And after I finished speaking, we embraced. There was a love in that moment that only a partner could offer.

**

I kept going to the group sessions that Father John led, but I still struggled. I just… didn't want to talk about these things in front of others. But my wife kept me going.

Father John could tell this struggle within was bothering me. He could see me wrestle with doubt, and my questioning a belief in a 'divine' being. I mean, who could allow so much darkness in the world. I'd lived with this darkness for so many years - looking evil in the face. I was trying to live in a normal world where so few could understand how 'we' have to hold a line of defense - how 'we' were the thin line that tries to keep society from harm... this was a struggle where not all of us survive.

How *was* I supposed to feel? My partner was the victim of such senseless violence.

 "My brother" Father John said: "seeing you struggle like this is, well - in a way like seeing a fish out of water. "What do you mean" I asked.

"You lost more than a partner that night" his voice steady but somber... "You were a victim too" he said.

Father John continued "you have a message, and the message - the words you need to say to others like you, are just as important to you as they are to the others - in group, or wherever you can find them."

Father John told me that I wasn't the kind of guy that was meant for speaking in church. He said the lessons I learned through my experiences were meant for those who were avoiding church.

He wanted me to find a little light in my life by helping others who needed "the light" - but maybe not religion.

I wasn't sure what he meant at the time, but he said "in time - I would"… then he just smiled.

**

My friends told me about a 'rally' some of the motorcycle clubs were holding. This meant we would meet at the motorcycle shop, and take a ride around the lake. They invited me to join in - knowing how much I still like to ride. Although I was still healing – I thought it might be good for me to get back out on the bike, and ride with some friends.

The following Sunday I met my friends at one of our favorite hangouts – a local café, so we could grab some coffee and some breakfast. After that, we rode to the motorcycle shop together. As we pulled into the parking lot - a couple of members from one of the biker clubs recognized me as a cop.

"I smell bacon" a couple of voices shouted out… all I could do is chuckle. I knew that it was all in good fun - the way bikers like to joke with each other. I parked next to my friends, and shut my bike down. One of my friends commented to the others that "he's no longer a cop - he became a Preacher!"

Several bikers chuckled while one hollered out "hey Preacher - Where's your Bible…" all I could say was "I'm really not a **preacher** - I spoke **one** time in Church - and believe me that doesn't make me a "Preacher?"

We all laughed…

As more arrived for the 'shop ride' - one of the other members of a club recognized me from a news article he'd seen… "Hey - aren't you the one who lost his K9 partner in that shoot-out a little while back?" he said respectfully… I nodded my head.

Some of the guys teased a little – "hey Preacher - why don't ya give us a Sunday sermon!" as they all laughed…

"You really want me to 'preach' to you?" I said with a chuckle, as I began my 'makeshift' sermon - I continued… "As we ride around the lake today – we all pretty much know where to go. So if you know where to go, and know the way to get there, you don't need anyone to tell you what to do. When one of us is in trouble, or when someone needs help, we band together to lift each other up… when one of us is hurting - we all hurt together… That's the code we live by - when one of us is lost, the others are there to show them the way. So I don't need a Bible, and I don't need to be a "preacher" - all I need today is to be here with you all."

Several more 'bikers' joined us - then a voice from the back of the pack shouted "now that's a Preacher I can listen to!" We all laughed…

Before we left the shop, a young man approached me. His father had been diagnosed with cancer, and he was afraid of losing his mentor and best friend. I told him, "Son, you need to be strong for him. He's going through tough treatments and will feel weak… he needs your strength."

"But what if I'm not strong enough? What do I do then?" he asked.

"You'll never know how strong you are… until strength is all you have."

As we talked, I realized these words came from a time when I was at my weakest - when I had to draw upon my own strength, and Bell's.

I shared some of my struggles, and the loss I recently faced, telling him that I doubted God. But I also told him that when doubt creeps in, we need someone to show us how to be strong.

The young man asked, "Do you think God tells you what to say?"

"I don't know," I replied, lighting a cigarette. "I'm not going to feed ya a line of 'bull-shit' and say I have all the answers. Maybe it comes from somewhere deep inside, from what I've been through… I just don't know."

He smiled. "You sure as hell don't talk like any preacher I've ever heard…"

"Well, I'm not a preacher," I said, seeing his puzzled expression. "I'm just another lost traveler, trying to find the right path. It's not about being a preacher – it's about helping each other find the path to where we want to go."

**

The rest of the day's ride was enjoyable - it was good for me to get out on the road. Even though the memories of loss - and of the pain are still fresh, it felt good to be with others.

Throughout the ride, and the gathering for lunch afterward, the only thing "they" called me that day was… "Preacher."

I knew it was all in good fun… and my wife, Bell - even Father John, saw the humor in it.

You wouldn't walk my path for a million bucks…

We do it…

For a lot less.

Chapter 2

Tina

A couple of days after I went out with the bikers, my wife and I were talking at breakfast, and she mentioned that Father John had asked about me when she went to church. She had told him what I'd been doing that Sunday, and he thought it might be good for me to talk about my experience. She passed along the message, but I was reluctant. I didn't even like talking about it in group – so maybe talking with Father John could be a better option, though I wasn't sure that was the right approach either. Sharing anything, whether in a group or one-on-one, felt difficult. But maybe Father John's invitation was something I needed to consider.

Later that day, while I was sitting on the patio, I was lost in thought, remembering Tina. I was still holding onto her leash, and her memory. Isabel told me I had a phone call. When I asked who it was, she said it was Father John.

I picked up the phone, and his voice was warm but steady. "Would you come by my office for a quick chat?" he asked.

I didn't know what to expect, but I knew I needed to go. I kissed my wife, slipped on my leather jacket, and rode down to the church on my bike.

I pulled into the parking lot, and the kids playing in the church-school playground all ran up to the fence to see what the thunder was, and it was only me. I got off my bike to see all the smiling faces and gave them a little wave of greeting.

Father John met me at the door - "it looks like you've attracted some attention" he said smiling. I smiled too, and thought to myself "I guess I wasn't the usual kind of 'parishioner' that shows up here at a church."

We sat in his office, and briefly discussed my day at the bike rally last Sunday. That's when I told him they were calling me "Preacher" – he thought it was funny. I told him that in spite of how good it felt, it didn't help - it didn't ease the pain as much as I thought it would.

"Acceptance" Father John spoke with a stoic voice with authority - "accepting what happened won't heal the pain, but it will open a path so you *can* heal... what we need to do is get you to be able to keep the fond memories, accept that you will have sorrow for her loss, understand that all the things you have experienced are a lesson, and that the pain you feel now, is not a life sentence." He went on: "the feelings of sorrow are normal, and I believe the anger isn't just about losing Tina, but the culmination of all the darkness you've seen through the years."

His words cut deep, and at that moment I told him that I'm not sure if I really do want to heal. I told him that healing might mean I don't respect her sacrifice - the sacrifice she made for me.

"I understand that my son" his face now turning back to his comforting smile... "So how about we start with you telling me a little about your partner - Tina."

**

"I remember the day I met her... I mean - I've had several dogs over the years – Shadow, Max, Ajax – not to mention Gunner from my Army days, but the police dogs were always adopted by my superiors when it was time for them to retire. It seemed they liked the way I cared for them, and how well they were adjusted to 'home' life… my wife said it was because I was a dog "whisperer." I believe it was because I'd learned how to speak to them - and to love them on a level of understanding - that could only come from a life where dogs were the only ones I could trust. It seemed like through my life - dogs were the only ones who could understand me too.

"I needed my next assignment to be a partner that could understand this as well… a partner who understood me as well.

"We were told that we'd be getting three new K-9's - and I would be getting my new "Partner."

"I was the Sergeant that supervised the K-9 crew - but the assignments were already made by our superiors. When the truck came from the airport, that the German based training company sent - the first dog to come out of the shipping crate was "Aries" - a black Malinois (*Mal-In-Wah*) – lean, mean, and lightning fast: right out of the crate he was ready for work… Aries was assigned to my corporal Stan - the football player – the Quarterback - and track star, who needed a dog who could 'keep-up' with him… smart and athletic - they were a good match.

"Next, out came "Thor" - another large mix between the Malinois, and a German Shepherd - black and brown - stocky and lean… living up to his namesake: powerful and commanding… assigned to my other corporal - Nick. Thor needed a handler who could 'pack the weight' - like the weight-lifter Nick was - who could carry a heavy load, and tackle big jobs… Thor was the right match for him.

"My anticipation was building - knowing what should come next would be another amazing specimen of German breeding… And out of the crate - stretching from the long trip… "Tina"

"She was sleek - smart, and had a look in her eyes as if she was wondering what kind of handler I would be. As if she was interviewing me for the job. We looked at each other - and she smiled at me, it looked like she said I'd be just fine. She was reddish-brown with a black saddle - her black muzzle graced her face with elegance, and she had a hint of grey across her back. From the start - I could tell we were destined to be together for a long time.

"She was different from the others - even Gunner, who I'd served with in the Army.

Right out of the 'crate' - she seemed like she knew "she was the boss"...

"She graduated from her training six months early - as if she knew what she was meant for. I discovered she could track, sniff, and it seemed she could find whatever it was I was looking for - even before I knew I was looking for it. It seemed like she had telepathy - a sixth sense - a "nose" for being a real cop.

"I told her to come, and instead of standing at "attention" like the other "military" trained dogs - she came and leaned against me as if she knew me from her beginnings. It was almost surreal - yet comforting... something about her made me feel at ease. Like a long lost friend coming home - something in my heart made me feel like she was home.

"I would learn so painfully later - how truly special she was.

"We all took a few minutes to 'get to know' our new assignments, and Tina was all too willing to get in my face, showing me the love from the start. She sniffed and licked me like we were 'old friends' reuniting.

"I asked her if she wanted to 'go for a ride' - and she paused, then looked around and started sniffing again. She jerked the leash out of my hand, and sniffing the ground - ran toward the K-9 Police truck that was mine. She jumped into the open door I'd left, and sat in the driver seat - smiling at me as I walked over – not too far behind her.

"Hey Princess" I laughed - "don't' you think I should drive?

"All the other officers laughed too - Stan said - "well Sarge - I guess she knows who's boss."

"On the way driving back to our home - I stopped and got myself a burger at a fast-food drive-in. As I was ordering - Tina, sitting in the passenger seat (instead of the kennel in the back of the truck), looked at me as if I should order her one as well… So I did. We sat in the parking lot and had our first meal together.

"As I introduced her to my family – it was like she knew what to do, because of what I was thinking. Tina slowly approached my wife, and as if she knew how to show Bell she wasn't a 'threat' - she lowered her head and nuzzled up against her feet. It was love at first sight. She immediately fit in to our family.

"Even the grandkids loved playing with her - and she was gentle, nurturing - and had the demeanor of a puppy. She could match the temperament of any situation, and as I would discover... she could bring fear to the Devil himself - when one of her 'own' was threatened.

"It wasn't too long after we got home that I took her outside with me, and I sat on the patio. I watched her play while I opened up the "personnel" file we got from the breeder, and trainers. I looked over at her, and then back down at her history page: the notes from the breeder *really* told the story..."

"Tina" the breeder wrote – "was the smallest of the litter, and showed from the start she was extremely intelligent." He wrote "I named her Tina since I knew she would be going to America, and because of her size being tiny - I thought Tina would be a good name for her."

The breeder - Hans - was bilingual, and noted further: "as I began her initial training before the

Schutzhund (protection dog) course she would be going to, I noticed that she needed very little training in the basic commands. She seemed to watch the others and know what to do. She was agile, intelligent, and very clever. She appears to have a good heart, and protective of her surroundings. She will make a good candidate for protection. In spite of her size she is muscular and strong."

"I read through the many pages - the notes from the advanced trainers, all of them amazed how special she was. Even they were amazed that she finished her training six months early... six months before her peers.

"I was lost in the reading, and before I knew it, she was sitting before me with a "what-ya-doing" look on her face. I smiled and told her that I was just getting to know her. The smile on her face said it all. She rested her head on my lap, and I stroked her fur, and I knew she truly was something special.

"She seemed to watch everything - and everyone - like she was always learning. She had her place in the house - her food and water dish - but she'd watch my wife get ice or water from the fridge door, and soon enough, she figured out she could get an ice cube to play with… or a cool drink of water… just by pressing the lever.

"It seemed like all she wanted was to be like us - until I'd find puddles of water and half-melted ice cubes on the floor by the fridge… nearly slipping on them more than once. I wanted to scold her, but I couldn't. I'd call her name, and she'd look at me - you know, with that 'I'm guilty' look with those big eyes…

"It was one of the best years of my career - and yes, I'm angry that it was all taken from me."

Father John interrupted gently, "How about we focus on Tina… not the anger."

Reluctantly, I agreed.

"I just feel so guilty Father - that I survived, and she didn't"

"I understand son - but tell me more about Tina"

I went on saying: "Her first day on the job was nothing less than what I'd read about her. From the 'get-go' she discovered drugs, and just her presence - when we needed a show of force, she could diffuse the tension – I guess suspects could tell that dynamite comes in small packages.

"Tina may have been smaller than a lot of her peers, but it seemed that she wasn't any smaller than a lot of the American-bred German Shepherds - anyway…"

Father John smiled and told me that 'it's all a part of remembering, and honoring her memory…"

I went on… "She didn't like riding in the kennel in the back of the truck - every time we would go to get in the truck, she'd walk over to the cab, and 'nose' toward the handle letting me know where she wanted to sit. Every time we got a call, it was as if she knew my call sign, and would give me the 'look' that she knew it was time for us to go to work…

"In all the time I've spent with these dogs - I'd never seen one like her. There was something about her that was - well - almost human. Not that I'm trying to put human traits on her, but she really seemed to know - to understand…"

"It really sounds like she was special" Father John said respectfully.

"Yes - she really was… the year I spent with her was more than remarkable - we grew to love each other. Not like a pet, but as a real partner. Every time we did anything - I knew I could trust her, and she knew she could trust me. I guess that's what hurts me the most. I feel like I let her down!"

Father John leaned back in his chair, his voice calm yet weighted with meaning. "It's clear Tina wasn't just a partner; she was a gift. She lived her life for you, gave you everything she had. What do you think she'd want you to remember most about her?"

I stared at my hands for a long moment before finally speaking, my voice low. "I guess… she'd want me to remember the way she lived, and not the way she died."

I leaned back in the chair, a faint smile tugging at my lips as memories surfaced. "Every morning, she'd nudge me awake before my alarm, like she couldn't stand the idea of wasting a single minute of the day. She was always so full of energy - she'd bring me her leash and look out at the truck, as if to say, 'Come on, we've got work to do.'"

I chuckled softly to myself "On patrol, she'd tilt her head whenever I talked, like she was hanging on every word. Sometimes, I swear she was more attentive than my team. And she had this thing with tennis balls…" My voice trailed off as I shook my head, smiling at the memory. "Didn't matter where we were or how serious the situation was - if she saw a ball, I knew she wanted to be all over it. It was like she was a pup again. But her training and dedication to her duty – kept her strong, but she knew - when she had the chance – she'd get to play ball…"

I paused again, my smile fading slightly as another memory came to me. "There was this one time I caught her sleeping in my chair - head back, paws dangling like she didn't have a care in the world. I thought about scolding her, but when she wagged her tail, I knew she had me wrapped around her paw. And she loved watching TV - especially when animals were on the screen. She'd perk up, ears forward, like she wanted to be a part of the show."

"One time – she heard an officer say the word 'drugs' on the radio, and she grabbed the mic, and started to talk – almost as if she wanted to make the call to respond – or the time we walked into the squad-room for pre-shift meeting, and she stole my chair from me, and sat in it like it was hers... she truly had the 'cop' sense of humor... and she knew it."

My voice softened again, as the weight of her loss came creeping back in. "Tina loved our little traditions, too - like sharing burgers and fries. She'd always try to steal a bite when I wasn't looking, but it was a game. She'd give me this look, like she was daring me to catch her. And then, there was that smile..." My voice broke slightly - "I'll miss that smile. She had this way of looking at me, like she knew exactly what I was thinking - and like everything was gonna be okay."

I fell silent, my gaze distant. Father John waited, letting the quiet settle between us. Finally, I spoke again, my voice barely above a whisper. "She gave me everything. And now she's gone, I let her down – like I let her go... just like that."

Father John leaned forward, his voice steady. "No, Jack. You didn't just let her go. She chose to protect you. That's what love does - it gives everything without hesitation. Tina wouldn't want you to carry guilt; she'd want you to carry her love."

I nodded slowly, the moisture in my eyes trying to escape - as I did my best to hold them back: "Yeah," I murmured. "She would."

The chat I had with Father John was more than a few minutes. It ended up being several hours, and when I walked away that day...

I was still angry.

"Where is the light that can reach

The scars left by the shadows?"

Chapter 3

Acceptance

Father John and I would talk for hours about Tina. He told me that moving past losing her didn't mean I should forget about her, but instead - keep her memory close... "She was loyal, she was courageous, and she protected you when you needed her" Father John continued... "Wouldn't the best way to honor her be to live the way you did when you were with her?"

"I don't know Father - if I didn't feel so bad, wouldn't that mean I don't respect what she did for me?"

Father John continued... "The pain and anger you feel, the feelings of sorrow - you don't need to hang on to all this to keep her memory – and her love for you... you see - your suffering doesn't come from the pain - it's coming from your *attachment* to the pain."

I disagreed with him... I realized that there are steps to healing like: denial, anger - acceptance, but I refused to accept that some 'scum-bag' took such a beautiful soul away from me.

Father John continued "it's common for different people to 'jump' around the different phases of grief" as he leaned back into his char - "like you holding onto her leash while you're out on your patio - in a way you are hoping to hold onto her - in a way denying that she's gone...

"Obviously you're angry, and I suppose it's okay for people to experience these different emotions at the same time." Father John leaned back in toward me: "No one can blame you for the way you feel - Jack, I just don't want it to consume you"

"I will never accept what happened" I blurted out.

Father John calmly replied "acceptance doesn't mean you approve of what happened, it just means you understand the reality that it *did* happen - it was a situation - a call that you couldn't control - it only means you can feel the sorrow, the loss, without letting it become suffering."

I told him that part of my anger comes from knowing that the world will never know how special she was - her selfless sacrifice - her true love for service. I told him that *he* may understand how special she was, but in the short time she was by my side - she touched the lives of so many… and I continued:

"A week into us being partnered - we got a call from the County Sheriff's department. They needed a K9 unit to help find a lost child up in the canyons. Tina heard our call sign, and she gave me the look, and I knew she was ready…

"At the campground where the Deputies were with the family of the lost child – we were handed some articles of clothing that they knew we'd need for Tina to track on…

"Tina could tell that the situation was urgent. Before I could get her leash on she acted like she knew why she was there - like I said - I believe she had a sixth sense about being a cop.

"I gave her the scent; she sniffed around the clothing, and pulled me over toward the edge of the campground. The Deputies said that 'wasn't the direction' they last saw the child' - but I trusted my little girl to do what she was trained to do.

"I had a hard time keeping up with her, and as we'd climb the hills in the steep canyon - she pulled me along, never breaking her pace. She would stop and lift her head - maybe even sniff the ground, and off she'd go - but all I could sense was the smell of fresh pine, and the damp woodland ground we'd been trudging through.

I was tired - it was starting to get late in the afternoon. Tina could sense the urgency, and I knew she wouldn't stop until she found what she was supposed to.

"We'd been hiking – running actually - busting through the trails and brush for a couple of hours - she stopped again, and raised her head again sniffing the air. Her ears started focusing on something - I could tell she heard something… we started to walk again toward a small clearing and then I heard it too.

"I could hear the soft crying of a child, and I told Tina she was a 'good-girl' as we walked closer to the sounds. We found the young boy huddled up against the base of a tree. I didn't want Tina to scare him, but before I could hold her back - she started licking his face, and nuzzled him affectionately around his neck. He stopped crying and asked me if I was going to take him to his mom and dad…

"I told him that 'we' were going to take him to his mom and dad, and I asked him if he was hurt - he said no, that he was just scared."

I continued to tell Father John that I radioed the others - that '*we*' found the boy, and that we were headed back. I took Tina off her leash, so I could carry the boy through the rough spots on the mountain side, and that Tina never left us - rather - guided us back down the mountain so I wouldn't get lost either." Father John smiled.

"When we got back down by the edge of the campsite - the boy's mother ran to greet us, and took the boy in her arms. The dad wasn't too far behind, and when he got to me - he threw his arms around me and told me that I was his hero.

"I told them that Tina was the hero. There was no way I could have found him - it would have been impossible for even a helicopter to see him... it was Tina that was the hero. The three of them hugged and pet Tina, and told her how much they appreciated her for finding their little boy.

"Tina got the reputation pretty quick around the department, that whenever they needed a dog for the tough calls - that Tina was the answer."

Father John said he remembered reading about this in the papers, and how impressed he was that the 'police dog' was able to find the kid in such open, and rough terrain.

He also understood why it was so hard for me to 'accept' her loss - but he wanted me to look at 'accepting a loss' in a different way… Father John said:

"Jack – you seem comforted when you talk about and remember Tina. You may not be able to change the facts - of what happened to you and Tina, but try to view it in a different way. If you can focus on the things you can control now, and use the logic in your mind to analyze what happened as if you are an observer" as he motioned his finger toward his eye… "Maybe it can open the door to 'not blaming yourself' for what happened - for not feeling guilty in surviving - when she didn't."

I sat in silence for a moment trying to understand… Father John broke the silence and said "you chose a life – a life where you are the protector, and Jack – that life comes with risks. Look back and think – what led you up to wanting to live a life where you knew you'd be in the middle of taking those hazards?"

"What made me want to be a cop? I guess I've always been drawn to protecting others, even if I didn't fully understand why. It's always been something I can't explain – like I was drawn to it. But something happened when I was barely a teenager – it's what made me become a good cop. You see Father - I had a secret spot - a hollow in the scrub oak between two hills we called 'pheasant hill.' It was the perfect hideaway for me and my friends to smoke, a place no one else could ever know about.

Getting caught would've meant the worst - my freedom, gone. But one day, while we were in our spot, we heard someone breaking through the brush. I was stunned to see a local cop, Officer Porter, standing there with a grin on his face. He asked what we had, and before I could respond, I handed him my pack of cigarettes.

"He took one, lit it, and smoked while handing me the pack. I thought, 'this guy's all right,' until he told me to crush the remaining cigarettes. He'd deal with the other boys later. Then he motioned for me to follow him to his car. I was scared now, as he gave me a ride home. I knew I had to think fast.

"When we got to my house, I walked to the driver's side and shook his hand. I thanked him quietly, but he nodded and told me to go talk to my mom. I told her I'd been riding around with him, avoiding the truth. She was suspicious about the cigarette smell, but I quickly blamed it on him – because I knew I could.

"A few days later, I saw Officer Porter's car again. He pulled over, and with a look, he asked if I wanted a ride. I got in, and we spent hours talking. I confessed what had really happened, when I talked with my mom - and he laughed. He knew I didn't have a father, and for years, he became that figure in my life - teaching me, guiding me. He even bought me my first leather jacket for riding my dirt bike.

"Through him, I learned that enforcing every rule wasn't always the priority. It was about building trust with the people you protect. One day, though, in the car, he turned serious and warned me: 'If you ever touch the *bad* stuff, you won't make it home to your mom.' I promised him I wouldn't, and I never did.

"Over time, Porter became a mentor. It was because of his example that I knew I wanted to be a good cop too. To protect, to be there for others - just like he had been for me."

Father John listened intently with a half crooked smile of his own then said "Jack – these are good memories for you; they carry meaning, and they can carry you forward. If you can reach into the past and remember some of these it can help soften some of the harsh. You may never fully 'accept' what happened to you, and Tina - and no one would blame you. Like I said - you have every right to feel angry" as his hands landed firmly on the rests of his chair - "we just need a way for you to feel peace as well, so the anger doesn't consume you. When you were young and in the 'infancy' of wanting to become a cop, you may not have realized all the dangers you'd face, but when you did, and when you faced the 'fire' – Jack – you never backed off… you rose to the challenge, and the challenge you face now is allowing yourself to live in peace. You did everything right, and you are not to blame."

I could understand what he was telling me in my mind, but my heart still hurts, and I refuse to 'accept' that she was taken away from me. I told

Father John that I can logically 'accept' the reality that it did happen, but not the sorrow and grief of missing her.

I was walking back out to the parking lot thinking about what Father John was saying. I thought "maybe he's right"... if I thought of my anger as a hardship, I could commit to making positive changes in my behavior - something like "fake it 'til I make it." But how... how do I pretend to be what I had a hard time accepting? What is it like to be a 'normal' part of the society - when all I've experienced is the worst of humanity?

I guess I would have to learn how to take small steps - and see each moment as an opportunity to overcome a challenge. I'm beginning to see that whatever it is that 'triggers' my feelings isn't the real problem. The real problem... was me.

While I was riding back home on my bike - I tried to think about the things Father John was trying to teach me. My thoughts kept creeping back to Tina, and how she was a comfort through the things we'd see, and how she was able to be a comfort for so many of the things I'd already seen. Maybe losing her also meant - losing a way to heal from a lifetime of darkness.

I was alone in my thoughts - thinking "I've lived so many years mired in the filth of the world, and so many of them were lived with a dog at my side. How can I be expected to accept these things? Things that aren't normal for most - were the experiences I could only hope to forget. I'm glad that I had so many good K9 partners to help me through these times, because I would never have wanted my wife to bear the burden of my experiences - even though she never would have complained about it."

I came home to an empty house, the silence thicker than usual, while my wife was on her shift at the hospital. I walked out to the patio; I lit a cigarette as I settled into the quiet with the memories of my youth still on my mind, and the longing for my partner still in my heart. In my hand, I held her empty leash, feeling its weight as if it held all the memories we shared.

Sitting alone, I let the silence wash over me, my thoughts circling back to her.

"I know, little girl… I miss you so much." My voice was barely a whisper, words dissolving into the evening air. "If there's any way you can hear me… please, help me through this. I know you're gone, and - God, if you're listening…

Let me feel her here with me just once more."

Chapter 4

The Rock

I was becoming more comfortable with Father John. And I was glad that Isabel had me talk to him. I still had reservations about letting anyone "in" – to see what was really happening inside me, or maybe I was having a hard time trusting anyone at this point… so – Father John, in his usual way of getting through the hardened walls I've built… asked me how my wife – Bell – how she was doing… even though I believed he already knew, he wanted me to think about all I'd been through and picture it in my mind – to see how it has been affecting her…

"I'm not sure if I understand Father – she's solid, and she's, well, she's always been there for me, and…"

Father John stopped me, and asked me to back up a little… "Jack, think for a moment – think for me, and tell me what it was like when – well –

when you first met, and how you two became a family."

I paused – took a breath, and while I looked out his window – past the tree and into the school play yard – my mind wandered back to that day… I smiled and chuckled, "I met her in a foreign country. I was a sergeant on a K9 bomb searching squad. My partner – Gunner, excited about 'the job' - jerked me as I held his leash and we'd jumped from a helicopter a little too soon, and I landed on my foot - just a little wrong. 'They' said I'd have to report to the medical unit before I could return to duty.

"Amid the organized chaos of a makeshift hospital, the smell of Army canvas protecting us from the dust we could never seem to escape… And there she was - blonde and beautiful. She looked at my sprained ankle, and as she moved it around, I winced in pain. "Don't be a baby about this Sergeant," she said with command - yet compassion - sporting a half smile and a slight chuckle "It only hurts for a minute…"

"I let her treat me, as if I had a choice, but as she fixed my hurt, she captured my heart."

"You're little friend here is beautiful" she said looking at my partner 'Gunner'... "He looks like he can 'hold his own'" she said with a smile.

"My K9 at the time was "Gunner." He was a large German Shepherd with muscles like steel. He - like most 'Shepherds' had a sense of loyalty unmatched by other breeds... He stood firm and stoic at the side of the bed where I was sitting, and watched her work on me with an intent look on his face - but still trusting, as if he knew - this 'person' - this "human" was someone - that if I could trust... so could he."

I smiled at Father John remembering Gunner: "he tried to help Bell when she was wrapping my ankle with an 'Ace' bandage, and she looked at him chuckling *are you trying to do my job for me too?*""

With a chuckle of my own I said "You know - 'Gunner' would like you to join us for a cup of coffee...?" I said questioning with a smirk, and a half smile...

"Yeah - I bet 'Gunner' would really love that" she smiled back with a wink in her eye. This was a smile that I would learn to love for more than 40 years...

"We had that cup of coffee, and a lot more. We learned that we could lean on each other in a place where trust, loyalty, and love were a luxury... and that finding that love in the dirt, dust, and sand of a foreign country... well - I knew that somehow... this would be a bond that would last forever..."

"Well Lieutenant" as I smiled at her - "Um - does this mean I have to salute you when we go out on a date?" I chuckled...

"You bet - Sarge..." she laughed. You better know who's boss over here" she smiled...

"That 'cup of coffee' turned into a lifetime together, and that mug of 'mess-tent sludge' turned us into a family. When we finally got the approval for the Chaplain to perform the ceremony – it was the three of us... Lieutenant, Sergeant, and 'Corporal Gunner' . . .

**

"It was a few years after we met, and after we'd left military service - I joined the Police force, and she started working in the local hospital's ER. I worked my way to become a motorcycle officer, and Bell worked her way into supervising other Nurses.

"Every morning when I would 'fire-up' my bike to go to work - she would pray - 'dear God - let him come home safe…' and of course - I would, but that never stopped her from worrying about me. All throughout the years there were times when I'd get home – well…" I paused for a moment, and then continued "there were those times, I would go to each of my kids' rooms, and make sure they'd be ok… my wife seeing this would ask - "how was your night…?""

"Do you really want to know?" I'd ask… and she'd calmly say - "no." Even though she'd seen so much over the years - as a nurse in the Army, and as an ER trauma nurse… I knew that she didn't need to hear about it all over again.

"If anyone would think for a second that the wife of an officer doesn't feel everything he goes through - is wrong!

"I could tell that every incident - every experience I went through, she felt - and somehow, she knew that every sight of a tragedy - the smell of death - the life I tried to hide from her, she experienced, and felt as much as I did.

"She didn't want to know, but I could tell she knew, and even felt what I was going through - she was right there with me. All she could do was hold me, and tell me that things would be all right.

"I would wake in the middle of a night with a bad dream, and she would simply hold me - comfort me - not knowing that the screams of a mother watching me put an eight-month old baby in a body bag still haunted me. That the smell of blood, and the sight of broken bodies still appear in my mind every time I closed my eyes...

"Somehow in the shadows of her mind - she experienced the same horror of my world, and the terrible things I would see - or feel, and even the memories I wish I could forget...

"Even though I don't want to talk about these things with her, my wife somehow knows - that the world I live when I walk out the door - is just as much a part of her life, as it is mine...

"When the call comes, and I don't know what I'm going to face when I get there - I have split seconds to make decisions, and keep control of uncontrollable situations. I have to make choices that will be scrutinized in reviews, courts, and opinions for months and years to come, but I have to do it in a half of a heartbeat.

"So when I'd come home after a shift, and she asks how my day - my night - or whenever it was I worked… I ask her if she really wants to know… and the look in her eyes tells me that she already knows."

**

"When I transferred to become a K-9 officer, I thought the horrors would end - that my new partner, Shadow, and I would just be finding drugs, contraband, and backing up other officers. But I was wrong. I ended up deeper in the world I thought I was escaping.

"Sure, there were rewarding moments - times when Shadow and I made a real difference in people's lives - but still, I had gained a reputation. When my partner and I showed up, it was because we were the ones called to solve the 'unsolvable' situations.

"No matter how hard the day had been, we'd come home to Gunner. It was like he had a way of teaching his new friend what to do - how to protect me, how to be 'on duty.' I've always been amazed by how dogs seem to learn from each other, as if Gunner was showing Shadow the ropes.

"I loved being a 'dog-cop,' and I loved working my way up to supervising them. Life at home was good, even with the weight of the real world pressing in. Our house was well lived-in, and the dogs adjusted beautifully to our growing family. They weren't just working dogs - they were part of our family, our protectors, and they were deeply loved."

It was a sad day when we finally put Gunner into memoriam, resting forever with us - as if watching over us… like the friend, protector, and family member that he was. He had been there when our family began, and now, in spirit, he would always be with us - a quiet guardian, still standing watch.

**

"Our years together only brought us all closer – all of us. We learned how to balance our lives – with work… so I thought."

"When I would come home from a shift – like all the others before her, I would take Tina's vest, her collar, and all of her gear from her, and let her know she was in a safe place... she would spend a few minutes out on the patio with me, and sometimes my Rock - my wife, would join us, and just sit with us... she would ask if I wanted to talk about it, and I would, but I knew she didn't really want to drag all the darkness of the world into our home. Even I didn't want to think about what we'd seen just hours before.

"I would say something like - it was a hard day, and she'd know that the horror's I saw would haunt her too. So I would sit with the 'girls' in my life, and appreciate that they both knew I just needed some time to decompress before the nightmares of my life would appear in the dark - when I closed my eyes in the embrace of my wife, and with the partner that slept at the foot of my bed, who was there too - to protect me as I slept."

"Keeping our work separate from home was never easy."

**

"My wife was my 'Rock' - she was the foundation I needed for me to keep my sanity. Even though I'd spent so many hours now in the 'group' and talking with Father John - it was the constant knowing - that the one who was there with me in the darkest of times, and through the darkness of the night, she was there to feel my pain - even when she didn't know the details of what I was going through.

"She had been through enough too, as a Nurse in the Army, in a combat zone herself. She worked in the ER at the hospital, and I knew - that she knew, and shared my nightmares with me."

**

Father John sat in silence, his face lost in the memories of his own... "I'm glad you have a foundation - a 'rock' that you can lean on" he said, "In many ways - I know how you feel."

I thought to myself - and I wondered how *he* could know how I felt... losing a partner was not something someone could understand... I asked him, but he already knew I needed to hear what he had to say... then Father John started to speak...

"My childhood buddy and I joined the Army on the 'buddy' program, and we went through basic training together, then we were assigned to the same unit when we went to Viet Nam. The jungles weren't like the fields we used to play 'Army' in back at home - it was a nightmare all our own.

"We were assigned to 'dig-in' to set a perimeter, and kept the enemy at bay for a week. One night we sat in our 'fox-hole' through the rain and the mud when the mortar shells started landing all around us." Father John, scratching his forehead, leaned back in his chair… "We tried to fire back, but it all kept coming. Gunfire and shells kept hitting us hard, and we did our best to keep them at bay.

"A mortar shell hit inside our fox hole, and machinegun fire kept us pinned down. Some of what I'm about to say was told to me by the men who were there with us… but,

"Both my buddy and I were hit - and hit hard. Everything went black. He tried to stop my bleeding - he did everything he could to save me. He held my chest wound tightly, and kept me from bleeding out. He couldn't move well through the mud, but he still kept me alive until the 'choppers' arrived to take us to the hospital."

Father John, was looking down at his feet, he paused, then returned his gaze into my eyes. "He ignored his own wounds, and kept his hands on my injuries. The medics wanted him to let me go, but he wouldn't. He kept his hand on my heart knowing that if he let go, I wouldn't survive. All through the flight to the hospital - he kept his hand right where it needed to be, so I could be saved.

"They rushed me into surgery, and they saved me. When I woke from it all, I asked about my buddy." Father John's eyes now staring off into the distance... "They said he didn't survive. He kept me alive in spite of his own wounds - he'd been hit in the femoral artery, and after I was cared for... he'd already lost so much blood... that there was nothing more they could do. He refused to let go of my chest wound - he sacrificed himself.

"I didn't just lose a partner that night - I lost a hero. I lost a friend I'd known since my childhood. It has taken me more years than I can count to realize I was not to blame for his death. He chose to live his last moments to save me."

As he spoke – my right hand tried to scratch away some moisture from the corner of my eye – then slowly as I lowered my hand to my chest – I could feel my own scars through my shirt – then I moved my hand down to my right leg, and I felt the scar through the cloth. As I felt the scar on my thigh through my pant leg – I realized now - how close I came that night Tina saved me.

"Yes - I felt guilty that I survived," Father John continued, "and he didn't. Yes - I felt the anger, the denial, I felt the grief that I'd never be able to say thank you… I've been there Jack - I've seen and felt, and known the loss that you are feeling.

"It may not be the same as what you are feeling, but Jack, it's as close as it can come…"

I sat there in his office stunned. We looked at each other for what seemed like an eternity. I could only say - "I didn't know what you've been through…"

Father John said that he doesn't like to talk about it either, but this would be a moment that he thought would be appropriate. He knew that I'd seen and been through a lot of similar actions when I was in Iraq and on the streets as a cop - he felt that he could share his experiences with someone who could understand.

As the hours passed that morning - we both cried together, and remembered our pain together. We both talked about the foundations - the Rocks that we leaned on when the pain of our pasts haunted our thoughts - the thoughts that become nightmares when the silence of the nights become the canvas that terror paints its indelible pictures, and the images we could only hope would go away - the images that reign heavy.

I knew from that day forward that Father John wasn't just looking to see me through my own fight, but looking in the mirror of his own past, and needing a friend that could understand the same things he was going through.

"Jack" Father John said softly as I approached the door to walk out... "The pain may never truly go away, but the thought I hold onto - similar to yours - is that my friend, my partner... will forever hold in his hands... *a little piece of my heart*."

**

When I got home from talking with Father John, I was met at the door to see the familiar silhouette of a woman with a smile standing in the doorway, and I knew by the look in her eye that she could tell I needed a quiet moment to just sit, and contemplate - to hold a hand. I looked deep into her eyes as she smiled that smile; the smile that said it all as she said "now you know why I'd needed *my* talks with Father John."

She seemed to know <u>what</u> I needed at the right time I needed it.

So we sat on the patio in silence together - both of us holding onto the end of an empty leash - a link that tied us to our memory - a lifeline that also, held us to each other - and to a love we *both* lost. It was as if the leash tied us to our Tina.

So many thoughts rushed through my head - Father John, Viet Nam, the night in the alley and the look in Tina's eyes... but - in that moment what I needed most was... the solace, and comfort of...

My Rock.

Chapter 5

Forgiveness

For several months - my meetings in 'group' went well, and my 'chats' with Father John continued. Every Sunday I'd go out for coffee or on a ride with my friends, and yet, slumbering still within – somewhere deep - I still felt the anger…

One evening sitting alone in my memories - on the patio… holding a leash… I heard the phone ring… my wife came out and handed me the phone - it was the Chief of Police. He told me that he wanted me to join them at the department headquarters for a memorial tribute for my K-9 partner. I was silent for a moment, as the flashback of that night hit me.

As I spoke to the Chief, the memory caught me off guard, clawing up from somewhere buried deep, surfacing in a flash. My heartbeat stuttered, and then slammed against my chest, fast and unsteady. Each beat feels like a hammer, jarring my insides, a sudden awareness that everything around me is both too real and utterly unreal. My skin prickled as if I was burning up, a hot flash that sends beads of sweat rolling down my neck. It felt like I was drowning, gulping for air that won't come, my chest a locked cage, I felt the scars of the bullets once again tightening around my lungs that just won't expand, and my gut - and the pain in my leg. I was there in the moment - yet watching myself as if from afar...

My mind is no longer in the present - it's back there. The images are too vivid: the sound of the gunfire, the yelp, and then the silence. Guilt wraps around me, whispering that it was my fault, that I should've done something differently. My stomach twists, and my hands shake, my fingers numb and useless. I try to press my palms together, to press the trembling away, but my mind is in freefall, scattered between past and present. I can't ground myself, I can't find solid ground. Every instinct screams to run, to escape - only there's nowhere to go.

Thirty years of training tells me to breathe, to center myself, but my body betrays me before my mind can catch up.

The world around me blurs, voices and faces melting away as if I'm looking through thick glass. My vision tunnels, darkening at the edges, and I fight to stay anchored, I fight to remind myself where I am. But the fear swells, thick and suffocating, as if all the air is being sucked out of the room. Just as my breath starts to ease, a tremor of shame washes over me, deeper than the fear, telling me I shouldn't feel this way – and that I'm supposed to be stronger than this. And yet, I'm paralyzed, caught in the grip of a memory too painful to bear.

Seconds seemed like hours, I fought hard to ground myself. I could hear my old 'boss' talking, but the words seemed like a blur... I had to interrupt him... I had to ask him to repeat himself... I lit a cigarette so I could regain my focus...

I was told the details for when I needed to be at the station. After I hung up the phone... It felt like I'd been hit in the gut.

I walked around the patio quietly - not knowing my wife had just called Father John. She'd sensed something was wrong as she overheard my conversation with the Chief, and... as always, she knew what I needed. She brought her phone out to me - told me who it was...

"Jack - I'd like to come over - you got a minute" as I thought Father John's conversations never lasted anything like a minute. I told him I'd be here, and he continued... "We have a couple of tough things I'd like to talk about."

"Great" I thought - the last thing I needed was anything 'tough', but I'd come to trust his judgment.

I opened the door and greeted Father John. Bell, ever gracious, cordially offered him a cup of coffee, and he - graciously accepted - then he asked if we could sit outside on the patio so we could - 'chat'.

"Isabel told me about the phone call," he said... "And I kinda knew it would be a tough one for ya Bud" his voice steady and calming. And he was right. I told him about what happened to me on the patio – how it felt like the world was caving in around me...

"I think you were having some sort of panic attack - and it's completely understandable. What you're going through, you need to share with those who understand. Jack, the world may not understand the pressures, the split-second decisions, or the constant threats of losing your life… but those you've served with do… and I really do think you should be there at the police station to honor Tina…"

I wasn't sure of myself again at the moment, and I didn't want all the cops I'd worked with to see any of my emotions. Father John said - "that's exactly what 'they' need… they need to see someone strong - **like you**, to show them it's ok for strong people - like *you* Jack, to be able to show emotions. That's what's kept you alive - your ability to show emotion, even though you've hidden it from others for so long…"

I knew that - like the rest of us who tried to live as "manly men" who could stand tall, and face the fears no one else could - that by holding back and not being able to release the emotions - sadness, fear, anger… that these could build up, and for some, could be dangerous. For me - it felt good to be able to let some of these things go, at least when I was talking with Father John.

"Jack, I think your next step is to learn how to forgive…"

I interrupted him - "I'll never be able to forgive that son-of-a-bitch for shooting us" the anger in my voice heating… Father John putting his hand on my shoulder simply said in his soothing voice: "I'm not telling you to forgive 'him' - I want **you** to be able to forgive yourself."

"Forgive myself? How can I forgive myself for what happened to my partner. How can I forget that look in her eyes as she lay in my arms - her life slipping away, and there was nothing I could do to save her... she trusted me - she needed me, and... she died saving me..."

Father John continuing softly said "You don't forgive yourself for being alive. You forgive yourself for thinking you *could* control what you never had power over in the first place."

"I should have protected her... I could've done more" I thought as the images in my mind, and pictures of that night rushed through my head... again.

Father John seemed to be able to see that I was remembering the thoughts of that night... and he continued... "You did everything you could, Jack. She knew that. The question is - when will *you* believe it?"

I sat quietly while I stared out at the horizon, lost in thought.

Father John took a deep breath and continued: "You aren't honoring her by carrying this guilt. She gave her life to save yours, and I'm sure she wouldn't want this to be the only thing you carry forward... Wouldn't she want you to live without all this weight on your shoulders?" Father John repositioned himself, settling back into the chair he was sitting on - a slight sense of him being uncomfortable... but he continued.

"Jack, do you remember when I told you about that night in 'Nam? About how **I** carried that weight for years, thinking it *was* my fault? It's not easy to let go, and I don't expect you to do it today... or tomorrow - but you owe it to yourself to start trying."

I shook my head, the anger still simmering "But how? How do I let it go when I can still see the look in her eyes, cradled in my arms - her life slipping away?"

Father John again placing his hand on my shoulder: "By accepting that you did everything in your power... and by honoring her sacrifice, and by living, and not by drowning yourself in this guilt."

I remained silent, my jaw clenched, fighting back the tears…

Father John went on - "Jack, I know that place you're in. But it's a prison we've built for ourselves. And forgiveness? That's the key to getting out. It wasn't easy for me either, but Jack… you're not alone in this…"

**

I arrived at the police station, feeling a knot in my stomach. I see my former colleagues standing in formation, their uniforms sharp, and faces somber. As I walk up to the podium, my heart pounds in my chest, feeling that familiar grip of guilt. It was how I remember standing in front of the congregation that Sunday morning. How I felt the pain of my memories, and how the guilt began to resurface then too. My wife sensing my hesitation squeezes my hand, and Father John joins us to stand by my side, offering a quiet presence of strength.

The Chief of Police takes the microphone first, his voice steady but emotional. He talks about my K-9 partner - her loyalty, her bravery, and her sacrifice. He speaks about how she saved countless lives through her service and how she gave her life protecting her partner... me.

As the Chief speaks, my mind drifts back to that night, the memory vivid and painful - my partner's eyes, the feeling of helplessness. But this time, the words of Father John echo in my head, pushing through the fog of guilt. "You owe it to her to live."

After the Chief finishes, a ceremonial tribute follows - a wreath placed before a memorial plaque with my K-9's name etched in brass. My hands are trembling as I'm called to speak. I don't know what to say. All I can think of is how I failed her.

I step to the microphone, the crowd - my community: neighbors, bikers and friends - strangers all watching expectantly. My voice is low at first, barely audible, but I force myself to speak.

"I... I didn't just lose a partner that night. I lost part of myself. And I've spent every day since then wondering if I could've done more. But standing here today, seeing all of you here today to honor her the way she deserves... maybe it's time I stop asking what I could've done differently."

My voice cracks, and I grip the sides of the podium as I gather myself "Maybe it's time I start remembering her for what she was - loyal, brave, and always by my side."

As I speak, tears well in my eyes, but I hide them. I know I should forget the adage that "Big-boys don't cry" – but I wasn't ready... I know this was for her – and maybe this was for me - the relationship we had, and the love we had for each other. At that moment, nothing else mattered, but I still held it in.

I look at the plaque, at my partner's name, her statue shining in the sunlight, and I feel the weight lift ever so slightly from my shoulders. For the first time, I allow myself to let some of the tears fall - not just for my loss, but for the release of all the guilt I've carried. I did my best to hide them behind the shade of my sunglasses, but those closest to me could tell…

Father John watches me closely, knowing this is a pivotal moment for me. My wife, standing nearby, takes my hand again, and this time I squeeze it back, feeling her support.

The final tribute is a salute, the officers all raising their hands to a gesture of honor. I stand straighter; I salute back, and let out a long breath I didn't know I was holding.

Afterward, as the crowd disperses, Father John walks over… "It wasn't easy, but you did it, Jack. And that's the first step toward forgiving yourself."

My voice still hoarse: "I'm not there yet, Father… but maybe, just maybe, I'm starting to see a way forward."

**

The drive home was quiet - words could not break through the feelings in my heart, and the silence now became a comfort. My Rock - my wife, never breaking her gaze upon me - simply smiling in a comforting way…

Entering the house - before I could even change from the retired uniform I was wearing… my wife - Bell… gently took my hand, and as we walked past the refrigerator near the back door, I looked at the floor – hoping just one more time, to see the puddles of water, and half melted ice cubes Tina would leave us… my wife sensing my nostalgia, held my hand tight and led me outside to the patio… she placed the end of a now vacant leash into my hand… and said softly… we'll hold onto this… all of this… together… forever…

As we sat in silence - there was a hint of comfort in knowing that there really wasn't anything else I could have done that night. I didn't know how to forgive, but I knew that by telling myself what happened wasn't my fault… was the first step.

I sat still, my back against the patio chair. I looked deep into Bell's blue eyes as the shadows stretched longer now, wrapping the landscape in a quiet that felt almost reverent. The ache in my chest hadn't gone, not entirely, but something else was there now - a flicker of peace, fragile but real.

For the first time in a while, I wasn't running. But I was still searching. In this moment, I was simply here, and that was enough - for now.

And then it struck me: the world I chose to live in had never promised certainty. The promise of safety? That promise falls on the shoulders - and hearts of the strong.

In that instant, I realized I would have to reach deep, into a place I thought was lost, to find the heart, the courage that...

Tina wanted to save.

Chapter 6

Trials and Testimonies

At times I look at my life - the same way a writer gazes at a blank page… wondering what words, wondering what thoughts, or what deep contemplations should be shared… and not sure of what the outcome will be.

But this page was different - the words and the message was clear. The time had come for me to appear in court. I read the court subpoena again - realizing how important it is for me to testify, so no one else would be hurt. It was my duty once again… to protect.

Many times I related the feelings of loss, of guilt, and anger - to those who could understand, but this was different. This time I would be telling about what happened to Tina – and to me - to total strangers. Firefighters, EMT's, Soldiers, and Cops - at least they could get a sense of what I'd experienced, but Judges, Lawyers, and Jurors may never know - or feel, the terror of being shot... of losing a loved one who served by my side.

I knew I needed some help.

My wife suggested I call Father John. She could tell that my actually having to relive the events of 'that night' would be different. I had to think...

I stepped out into the sunlight and sat for quite some time thinking - "this isn't about my feelings - this is all about the facts. This is about putting a criminal away for a long time."

**

I sat in his wooden chair, and I gripped the armrests, nervous - knowing that what I was about to talk about would be the hardest thing I could do. Father John sat across from me - close, so I could feel the comfort he was there for. Although Isabel was my 'Rock' - my soft place to fall - Father John was a comfort that only a trained counselor could provide.

"Jack - I know this will be hard, and hard times call for tough men. We've talked a lot about this, but in a way - danced around the details of what actually happened that night."

"I know" I said looking deep into his eyes, "and I don't know if I'm really ready to do it" as my eyes now drifted toward the trees - the playground outside Father John's window... looking at the innocent children - the lives that should never know horror...

"How about you tell me what you were doing as you were getting ready for your shift that night" he said peacefully, yet commanding. And all the memories of that day – the day that turned into the darkest of nights... began to play like a broken film reel, scenes flashing out of order - overlapping, pulling me in without warning.

Father John gently rested his hand on my knee: "Jack - let's start with the simple things - take a deep breath, and describe your routine of getting ready..." and I began again...

I looked around the room - then back out the window, and the pictures I saw in my mind, it was a beautiful day. "I was outside sitting on the patio. I can see my wife walking out to the patio with Tina by her side - both smiling, and they joined me for coffee."

"Then" I continued... "It started like any other day. Working the swing-shift always seemed exciting - and we got to see both daylight - and nights... and it gave us the time before we went to work to play with Tina for a few minutes... I wish I had those minutes back...

"It was a quiet routine, the familiar motions. I knelt beside Tina, securing her vest, checking the straps, making sure everything was in place. She always stood still for me, patient as always, her dark eyes watching me with that steady calm I'd come to rely on. My hands moved from buckle to buckle, more out of habit than thought, but tonight felt different. I would always put her duty collar on last - like I was putting on her necklace. I called it her 'pretty'... she would smile.

"You ready, girl?" I said in a low voice, giving her a light pat on the side. She responded with a small pant, her eyes full of loyalty and focus. She knew the drill. This was what we did. Day in and day out, we prepared for the worst, knowing it could come at any moment – praying it never would.

"I went out to warm-up the truck, while my wife sat with Tina on the patio, and when I walked back to them they were getting in one last 'hug' before we all went to work…

"*You look after him*" she told Tina standing up to kiss me good bye. "*You take care of 'our guy' Tina*" she said with a bit of nervousness in her voice. We all walked toward the truck, I opened the door and Tina jumped in with her usual joy of 'going for a ride.'

"It's hard to explain how you can have a 'routine' day and yet feel a kind of heaviness in the air, something I couldn't quite place. We'd been on several searches for drugs, a number of traffic stops, and stood ready to back up some officers on a domestic violence call." I chuckled slightly: "Tina had a way of diffusing a situation, just by her being there."

"Tina had her favorite burger joint, and she loved French fries. I radioed into dispatch that we'd be stopping for our 'lunch' break - even though it was approaching 8pm in the evening. We picked up our food, and pulled through the parking lot where we could eat under the lights, as the day drew on becoming darker.

"I turned my radios down so we could eat in peace for a minute, when my Corporal - Nick, pulled his truck up to mine - so his driver side window was next to mine. He told me that he'd heard on the radio there were a couple of fugitives from the next State over, 'that they were armed and dangerous,' and that their last know direction was up the Interstate toward us. I turned up my radio so I could hear the "attempt to locate" call - I wrote down the description of the suspects and their vehicle. Everyone on my team let dispatch know that we 'copied' – in other words, we received the message.

"Tina - alert as ever seemed as if she knew what to be on the look-out for too…

"I thought I'd take a slow drive up by the foothills overlooking the city, just to see if I could see anything out of the ordinary. "Bell called me from her work at the hospital just to see how things were going: I knew she felt a sense of nervousness, and was curious if anything was out of the 'norm' - I joked with Tina while I was on the phone with my wife, asking Tina if she "saw any 'bad-guys' and Tina would get that 'excited' look on her face. My wife laughed, and I told her I'd call her back in a while.

"Tina and I parked on a hill overlooking the city. I turned off the truck and lit a cigarette, watching as Tina wandered around for a few minutes. The radio was turned up just enough to catch any calls, but for now, it was just the two of us, sitting under a cloudless sky as the stars brightened above. If there was ever a moment to hold onto forever, a night meant to etch itself into memory - this was it. Or at least it should have been.

"Tina eventually came and sat beside me while I finished my smoke. We didn't speak; we didn't need to. For a few fleeting minutes, the world faded away, leaving only...

Tina and me.

"Not seeing anything up in the hills - we made our way back down toward the city lights. By now we heard several officers in another division call out on the radio that they thought they saw the suspect vehicle down in the industrial district. So I told Tina that we'd go take a look with them. She looked excited.

"We didn't get too far before the other officers called out that they confirmed it was the suspect vehicle, and now a possible visual on at least one of the suspects. I used the "car-to-car" mode on the radio to let both Nick and Stan get their dogs Thor and Aries ready to respond. We pulled into a warehouse complex, as more officers arrived. I was the ranking officer so I directed some to set up a perimeter to block anyone from leaving, and the others to block off the alley-way where they spotted the suspect. I motioned for Stan to follow me over to where the suspect vehicle was…

"Tina and I pulled up and got out - Nick and Thor not too far behind us. I told Stan and Aries to set up on the entrance to one of the alley ways thinking if anyone were to 'run' they'd be the best at catching them. Stan looked at me and smiled saying *go get 'em Sarge - you two make an awesome team*."

Nick and I parked our trucks so we could block anyone from leaving also, and more officers began to arrive. I told them to hold their position at the entrance.

"Nick, Thor, Tina, and I started to walk slowly up into the dark alley. Nick commented quietly '**most people wouldn't go in here for a million bucks... we do it for a whole lot less**' - and he is right. We continued to walk slow - quiet - the dogs panting in anticipation. Out of the corner of my eye I saw movement, I ordered the individual to '*STOP! Get on the ground*' but he didn't. It looked like he was reaching for a weapon and Nick let Thor loose. I held Tina back - in full attack mode - while Thor made one huge leap and tackled the suspect, who did have a weapon in his hand at this time.

"I immediately called out on the radio 'roll medical' so we could have an ambulance on hand to treat any wounds Thor might leave on the suspect. I could hear Thor's excitement and the suspect's pain. Nick told Thor to stop, and for the suspect to get face down on the ground. Nick kicked the pistol away and Thor stood close as Nick started to cuff...

"I told Tina to 'sit-ready' - while ordering a couple more officers to help take the suspect into custody, and walk him out of the alley - Thor still ready and watching the suspect, bearing teeth... Tina ever more vigilant scanning the darkness for any more threats.

"I looked deep into the darkness, then down at Tina, the hair on her neck raised and her teeth ready - I knew she could tell something was down the alley hiding in the dark.

"The first suspect was in custody" some officers said over the radio - I could hear them talking to the suspect as they walked him back toward the opening of the alley - asking him where the other guy was - he just laughed. Tina, and now Thor, both gazing off into the darkness - the only lights coming from our vehicles parked a hundred feet away.

"I asked Tina - *'what do ya see little girl'* and she started tugging at her leash. *'Hold tight girl'* my hand slipping down to the clip that restrained her on her leash. Slowly releasing her - she stayed at my side - I told her to 'heel'… we took a few steps, slow and steady - and I drew my pistol from the holster as we inched further into the alley.

"I was in the lead, and hearing Thor panting in a near frenzy, I knew Nick wasn't far behind me."

I told Father John - still listening intently, that it is impossible to describe the surreal - to see, hear, and feel - even smell everything going on - to describe the indescribable…

"Do your best Jack" he whispered…

"Tina and I take a few more steps - I'm trying to make sense of the shapes - the shadows - can I see any movements? A few more steps… I hear nothing but my heartbeat - dogs panting furiously… I see the brilliant flashes from the muzzle of a rifle. I fire my pistol at the flashes. It feels like someone hit me in the chest - then again in the gut, like getting hit with a baseball bat - my right leg feels like it's on fire. I feel the concrete on the back of my head as I hit the ground… but I turn toward the flashes from the rifle and fire my pistol again and again while I feel Tina dragging me by the collar of my ballistic vest - tearing my shirt - I see Thor rush through hail of bullets. I can hear the screams of a man amongst Thor's growls.

"There's a torrent of radio calls - shouting, while a lot of officers now rush to help. Tina lay across me - then I sat up against a building - behind a garbage dumpster, Tina now in my lap. I could tell she was hurt - I started removing her gear. I moved my hands up and down her - now covered in her blood. I couldn't breathe - it hurt. I grabbed Tina and held her close, her breathing was fast and I could tell she was in pain.

"I kept telling her *"you're going to be fine girl"* as I stroked her hair: *"we're going to get you taken care of."*

More and more officers came, and I could hear some of them saying they needed several more medical teams – *"Officer down"* and *"the suspect is down"* – but I ignored them. My mind was focused on Tina, I couldn't breathe, but I kept talking to my Tina - *'I love you girl - mamma loves you - hang in there baby, you're going to be Ok*!' I struggled for a breath - I looked deep into her eyes - once dark - yet bright, now fading into the darkness that surrounded us. Her breathing slowed, and her eyes closed as we looked at each other for the last time."

As I spoke my eyes were closed envisioning the moment.

**

As I opened my eyes – I was now sitting in a chair that has no arm rests. The pictures of that night were still flashing before me in my mind. I look across the large room to see Father John and my wife Isabel sitting in the audience. Tears in their eyes - tears in the eyes of the jury... my heart pounding - I knew that I had to be at my best. There was too much at stake. And all I could hear was the Judge saying...

"Answer the question sir..."

"No" I said: "there was no one else in the alley that night. After the first suspect was in custody - there was no-one else, but the other officers, and (me pointing at the defendant) him."

I looked at the defense attorney - my heart still pounding, and he stared back at me. I could feel my anger, I could feel the loss all over again, but I wasn't going to break. And all he could say was... "No further questions."

**

We walked out of the courthouse that day - silently, in near reverence. Now standing in the sunlight, Father John said "I know it wasn't easy, but I'm proud of you." Father John turned to my wife Bell and said: "I know this wasn't easy for you too."

Bell looked at Father John with a faint smile, "Thank you for being here, Father John... for him, for both of us." She took my hand as we walked - her touch a steady reminder that through all the trials, the darkness, and the loss, she was my anchor.

Bell was at work that night - she was there to see first-hand what had happened to me... she was the first one at the hospital - to treat my wounds.

I could tell this was a nightmare she had to relive as well. But she stood at my side quietly and embraced me, and said "you were so brave - I'm proud of you too."

As we reached the parking lot I was able to take a deep breath feeling the weight lift from me - even if ever so slightly. The trial was over, but the memory would never fade. The sacrifice Tina made was one that I would carry with me forever, her loyalty etched into my soul.

For the first time since that night, I felt a bit of peace knowing that justice was served, even though it came at a cost I'd never fully heal from. I looked up at the sky, and with a faint whisper on my lips I said, *"Rest easy, girl... we did it."*

Father John was right - I wasn't walking this path alone. With us at the courthouse were so many of the Officers who were there with Tina and me that night. All of them in their 'Dress' uniforms - pressed and polished; a testament to the unity that brought me through that dark night.

Before I could reach my truck to drive home, they formed a line for us to walk through, and in unison as my friend Stan shouted "Present-Arms" they snapped to 'Attention,' saluted sharp, and remained steadfast as we arrived at my truck.

I turned… and with the moisture from my eyes hidden behind my sunglasses – I returned the salute as they snapped their arms back to their sides. I *shouldn't* have cared at that moment - to even *try* to hold back the tears, bit I did - because…

"Big boys - aren't supposed to cry."

"If you know how to listen to the wind...

You are never alone"

(Native American saying)

Chapter 7

Sheepdogs and Wagon Wheels

The days following court – and having to relive that once bright day that turned into the darkest of nights - were filled with a mix of emotions, swirling through my mind, and landing in my heart. Anger, sorrow, guilt - confusion, all spun together cementing the indelible picture in my mind - of my last look at Tina.

I tried to shake it all off - I struggled to process it logically, but nothing seemed to work. Isabel, always intuitive, suggested we take a ride together to help clear my mind.

We ended up in a small countryside town hosting a Border Collie competition. We watched herding trials, obedience tests, and agility courses. I watched these magnificent animals, listened to them bark - laughed at their playful antics and endless energy. They seemed to enjoy the open air and sunshine as much as me.

I looked at Bell; I said "The dogs - they move with precision, focused and unrelenting, their eyes never leaving the flock. It's like a dance of instinct and purpose." The hum of the crowd, and dogs barking all seemed to fade into the background as the moment shed a spark - a flash of clarity. As if by some sort of inspiration on why Bell brought me here today… it hit me. I wasn't just impressed by their ability, but it struck a nerve about my own life. The dogs I watched that day weren't just moving sheep from one point to another - they were protectors.

I sat there, reflecting: *I'm a Sheepdog.* I've spent most of my life guiding the flock, keeping them organized, helping them get to where they need to go. I was just like them - I had a duty to watch over my community - my flock… standing between them and danger.

Sometimes, I would have to bare my 'Sheepdog' teeth, and fight the fight; I had to deal with things the flock - my community - couldn't handle. But then I would quietly retreat to my safe place, my Rock, and like - how a sheepdog would lick their wounds, I would prepare for another day.

My wife seemed to sense the thoughts deep in my mind, and asked me softly if I'd ever thought about getting another dog. The idea brought a pang of fear - of losing another partner. It nearly sent me into a panic. Then she said quietly, "You know... you weren't the only one who lost a partner that day."

Her words hit me like a blow. Bell had been going through the same pain I was, and it should have brought us closer - like Father John's understanding had - but it didn't. She may not have been in the line of fire, but she had been my foundation, the one pulling me through, treating my wounds. And when she needed my strength, I wasn't there for her.

For Bell, that night wasn't just about losing Tina. She almost lost me. The realization struck me deeply. She had saved my life, and treated my wounds - all while knowing Tina wasn't coming home. I couldn't imagine how unbearable that must have been for her.

"I'm sorry," I said at last. It was all I could manage. All this time, I'd been mourning Tina, consumed by my own loss. Maybe it wasn't selfishness – maybe it was, but I had been so caught up in my grief that I'd missed the signs - missed what my wife was going through.

**

Meeting with Father John was more than therapy. He was not only curious about my going out on rides with my 'biker' friends, but also how I was doing with the anger, the guilt, and blaming myself for what happened. He knew some of my friends were in the same PTSD meetings I was going to. I told him that I didn't feel ready to share *all* the things I'd experienced to them - the way I was sharing with Father John.

I told my friend - my counselor, that my wife mentioned getting another dog. I told him that I was afraid of loss - getting attached and missing another relationship... I told him that I now realized that my wife too missed and mourned my partner... our partner. I told him my heart nearly 'skipped a beat' when she asked me about having another dog. I told him that thought made me feel like I would be replacing Tina... replacing her memory. And all those feelings – and, well - they brought back the memory of the pain.

Father John said "it's normal for innocent comments to 'trigger' emotions – feelings and such, and there are probably a lot of other things too… things that can spark some of those memories – experiences of your life 'on duty' – that you're trying to forget. Jack… there are lots of things, and even combinations of things that can 'trigger' you back to that night."

I nodded my head – because in my mind, and as I thought - I wasn't just agreeing with what he said, that it wasn't just simple words or comments, but I was remembering things like sights, or sounds, and even the smells… and for a moment, and before I could break the silence - as I paused - my voice cracked a little: "The wail of sirens that echoes in the distance, sharp and insistent, those sounds pierce through the quiet of my time out on the patio. It seems like the sounds of the sirens snap me back to that day - the day everything changed. The bullets, the shouts, the blood - my partner, gone in a flash of violence. The loss always fresh again, like an open wound I can't stitch closed… Father - I can still feel the heat of that moment, as if it were happening all over again."

Pictures in my mind flashed again – even the pain I tried to ignore as my partner closed her eyes… I felt it all over again, and it was hard to speak, but I went on… "The sirens… whenever I hear them in the distance – they still take me back to that night. They trigger me back to the smell of blood. Even now, I can almost taste it, thick and metallic on my tongue. You know Father - they tried to prepare us when we were in the Police Academy - for the sights and sounds… they showed us pictures of shattered glass and twisted steel, and even pictures of crime scenes and such… but no one could ever prepare us about the smells, no matter how hard they tried. These smells are what worm their way into my nightmares, creeping into my senses when I least expected it. You can't escape it."

The priest nodded with understanding in his eyes. "'Triggers' come in many forms, Jack. Sometimes it's what you see; sometimes it's what you hear. And for you... it's all this, and much more – it's also about what you smell. We can't run from it. But we can learn to live with it."

Father John leaned back into his chair and gave me that smile of his and continued: "Jack – let's take a step back, and think about your day at the Sheepdog competition. You were enjoying the sunshine, the dogs – just having a good day with your wife. I'm sure you were thinking about

Tina, but you had moments where the memories weren't as painful – didn't you?"

"Yes Father – I guess so" as I thought back… "It really was a good day for me…" I went on and told him how sorry I was for not realizing how much Bell was going through. I felt bad it hadn't dawned on me.

Father John wanted me to focus for a minute, just on me though… "Jack – I know it's not easy, but let's go back and talk about some of these things that 'trigger' you into the memories that cause you pain…"

Father John said that "it's normal for comments – or other sounds to trigger memories, and that one trigger – as simple or 'innocent' as it may be, can set off many others…" he went on… "Trauma - PTSD, and other feelings, are like the spokes in a wagon wheel, leading back to you Jack - the hub, the same place where all the pain lived. Everything connects" - his voice was steady, his hand tracing a circle in the air as he went on…

"Memories, trauma, fear – they're all part of the wheel. And right now, you're stuck in the center of it, with all those spokes pointing inward. But healing, Jack, it's about finding a way to deal with each spoke - each trigger, one at a time - and isolate them from letting 'em consume you."

I sat quiet, my imagination painting a picture in my mind - me standing in the center of a large wagon wheel - the spokes pointing inward toward me - sharp and threatening... I didn't like it... I forced my attention back to listening to Father John as he continued:

"The memories of loss, of any - or even all of your experiences will never go away, but what we need to do is keep it from dominating you, controlling you - damaging you. We need to find a way to turn your focus on the things preventing the trauma all around you from getting to the center - to you."

He leaned forward slightly "Jack – I think I have an idea that may help..."

As he spoke, I was deep in my thoughts - I couldn't help but reflect on how many jumbled memories flooded me... the pictures during my academy days - crime scenes, mangled cars, and lifeless bodies - enough to think I'd be prepared for the real thing. But what no one warned me about, what no training manual could explain was the smell. The copper tang of blood hanging thick in the air, mixing with burnt rubber and gasoline. It was a smell that clung to me, that soaked into my skin and followed me long after the scene was cleared. No textbook mentioned how the scent would latch onto my memory like a vice, showing up in the most unexpected moments, even years later. Nothing I could do - would, or could, let me escape the sensations that haunted me. Memories and nightmares that lurk in the shadows of "our" minds, that all too often drown those of us who haven't sought the solace of a lifeline…

My thoughts drift back to that night – every time one trigger 'hits' me – others follow. And it seems that these triggers – lead to me remembering the smell of blood – and keeps "that night" fresh in my mind.

"I'd learned and experienced and I thought I was prepared for the worst - and in many ways - I lived through it all." It was hard, but I tried to keep my thoughts focused. "I'm sorry Father - I'm having a hard time focusing…"

"It's Ok - believe me - I understand..." Father John smiling in an understanding way...

"How do I get past all the 'triggers' - how do I keep from alienating Isabel - I know she's paying the price for all this - how could I even make it up to her?"

Father John looked deep - studying my face "One step at a time Jack – you're not going to be able to make anything up to Bell, until you learn how to help yourself."

"I feel so bad - I feel so angry - angry that - that 'ass-hole' shot my partner..." I could feel the anger welling within me... Father John went on and explained why losing Tina - in a way 'broke' me... when I'd been through, seen, and survived so much. "I don't know Father - maybe losing Tina was the final straw that broke the proverbial camel's back?"

Father John spent a few minutes going back over how losing Tina was the pivotal moment that brought a lifetime of trauma to the surface. The look in Father John's eyes told me he had an idea... but he told me to continue – he wanted me to 'get it out' in the open – for me to express feelings I'd held inside… for so long.

"I don't blame the gun - I don't blame the bullets that ripped through my body - I blame HIM - he shot my Tina" my voice raising… "He is alive - I am alive, and my Tina - she'll never see another sunset. She'll never play with her toys, or feel our love! Father - she is gone! Father - my Tina - she's gone" as tears began to well-up from my eyes… "I was able to save Gunner, but I couldn't save Tina!"

Father John was able to understand as no other could in the moment. And as we talked - he was able to relive his own pain as he'd shared with me before… he wasn't just an educated, trained counselor and therapist… in this moment, he was my mentor… he was my friend.

As he was able to calm me - we talked further so I could identify and then isolate the triggers… triggers that could be something as simple as **me** complaining about idiot drivers on the road, to the sights, the sounds… and the smells that bring back vivid images of horror… how many searches found lifeless bodies – how many rescues had failed. There are too many crashes –

too many homicides, and so many times a routine day becomes a nightmare '**we**' have to bear the burden for. I told Father John that I couldn't even watch a mother stroll a baby down the street without remembering the screams - the memory of a crash, and having to take a lifeless baby from a young mother's arms… and place it in a bag…

As we talked, we painfully remembered so many 'trauma's' that surrounded me, and that they may never go away, but we could at least deal with each one independently.

"You see Jack – you've been trying to deal with all of these triggers at once – whether you realized it or not. This is why I want you to be able to identify each one as separate, so we can find a way to replace each of them with something good – like how you could remember Tina without the pain while you were watching the Sheepdogs out in the countryside."

Father John's words sank in deeply, but what hit hardest was his analogy - the wagon wheel. Each trauma, each trigger, was like a spoke connecting back to the hub, to me, to my core. It was all connected. But his calm voice carried hope, even when I felt overwhelmed by the weight of everything.

I sat in silence for a moment, thinking about the Sheepdogs I had watched that day in the countryside. They weren't just herders, guiding the sheep from one place to another; they were protectors. They stood between the flock and whatever threat might come from the wild - watching, waiting, always alert. That's what I had always been - a Sheepdog, standing guard, baring my teeth when needed. But it hit me then: just like those dogs, I wasn't just protecting others. I had to **protect myself**, too.

Father John had traced those spokes of trauma back to me, to the hub. But maybe part of being a Sheepdog wasn't just only about fending off the wolves. Maybe it was about finding a way to shield myself from the things that threatened to break me down. I realized it wasn't just about the bullets that nearly killed me, or the blood or the horrors I'd seen. It was the triggers, the things that kept gnawing at me - the sounds, the smells, the memories that were a constant reminder of each day on the job could be my last. These triggers – they'll never go away. They're always around, and they're a constant reminder that brings back the pictures in my mind… They were the wolves at my door. And if I didn't find a way to fend them off, I'd be overwhelmed.

Father John leaned forward - his face turned from the stoic understanding stare back to his slight grin, and he simply said: "The Sheepdog stands firm, protecting the flock, but even the Sheepdog needs moments of rest, moments to recover and heal. It doesn't mean they stop protecting. It means they become stronger, more resilient, prepared to face the wolves again tomorrow. Jack – the Sheepdog knows the threats, knows the danger, and knows that each day could be its last, but it also knows how to celebrate each day as a success – how each day is a victory over the adversary. Jack, that's where you are now."

I needed to become that kind of Sheepdog again. Not just for the flock, but for myself - and for my wife, my Bell. Father John was right. I couldn't protect her from my pain, or from our loss, until I found a way to protect myself from it first.

"I'll keep fighting," I said softly, more to myself than to Father John. "I'll find a way to deal with it… the triggers… the memories."

"You will," Father John replied. "One spoke at a time, Jack. I want you to come by tomorrow – you've made a lot of progress in conquering your pain and your fear of loss, and even the anger... I'll see you tomorrow."

As I left his office, I thought again of the dogs in the field -watchful, steadfast, and protective. And for the first time in a long while, I felt like I could be a Sheepdog again.

I walked in the door and saw my wife in the kitchen, and I looked at her - I paused... I held her close, feeling a new resolve settle in. I wasn't alone in this - she was my strength, my purpose. I needed her - so - together; I'd find my way back.

I felt a surge of pride I thought had been lost forever. Yes, I had been broken. Yes, I had been beaten. But as we stood there together, I understood - survival wasn't just about enduring. It was about recognizing my victory, and reclaiming my life, one step at a time... one spoke at a time.

We stood side by side, our words unspoken but clear in the quiet connection between us. My thoughts of how she not only cared for my wounds, but how she - in many ways...

Has held my heart in *her* hands.

Chapter 8

Hands

The following day when I met with Father John, he asked me about my day - handed me a cup of coffee, then had me sit in a chair unusually close to his. I wasn't totally surprised, but not sure what he had in mind. Father John asked me what religion meant to me. And I told him that I wasn't sure if religion *was* really meant for me. I reminded him of my doubts – "I mean, how could God let so many bad things happen...?"

"Ok Jack" Father John said with a smirk - "I can understand that. I know - well - knowing that you've experienced a lot in your life, I'm not going to give you a 'Sunday School' lesson, but I want you to think about something..."

I still wasn't sure where he was going to go with this, but I said "I'm listening..."

Father John continued: "as you think about *you* as the hub of our imaginary wagon wheel, and the spokes bringing all of the trauma you've experienced - the trauma that's surrounded you - directly to you... if we can replace each of the spokes - each bad memory with a good one – that's where I'd like to start…"

I was interested - and yet doubtful, and Father John went on… "Let's take a look back at the day you and Bell were watching the Sheepdogs – this was something that brought you joy - instead of the something that brought you pain. Even though you could still think about Tina – it didn't remind you of the anger you feel…"

We sat for a few minutes - my mind swirling with memories, both happy and sad. Moments that made me smile - even laugh - drifted through my thoughts.

"It's kind of funny, Father," I said with a small smile. "She'd lose one of her favorite balls and come tug at me, almost trying to tell me to follow her so I could fish it out from behind a cabinet or somewhere she couldn't reach - how she would almost try to verbalize that she wanted me to follow her." I paused, my smile fading. "It's hard sometimes… the things that make me happy are the same things that remind me of what I've lost."

"Jack," Father John said quietly, "that's normal. But what we've got to do is focus on the happy parts - it's all right to feel the loss too."

Father John continued, leaning in slightly, his voice calm and reassuring. "Jack, it's normal for the happy memories to also carry a sense of loss. It's part of the human experience. But here's the thing - those moments of happiness still have value. They shaped you, and gave you strength. We can't erase the pain, and the anger may never completely go away, but we can make sure it doesn't overshadow the joy. Just like you did the other day."

I nodded slowly, but the doubt still lingered in the back of my mind. "I get what you're saying, but it feels like every time I try to think about something good, the bad creeps in. I don't know how to separate the two."

Father John smiled softly. "It's not about separating them, Jack. It's about learning to hold them both at the same time. Life is a mixture of joy and sorrow, and one doesn't cancel out the other. Think of your hands... one holds the joy, the other holds the pain. You don't need to choose between them, but you can learn to let the joy shine a little brighter."

Father John reached over from his chair across from me, and took me by the hands - I felt a bit uncomfortable, and yet at the same time, comforted… and he went on…

"Jack, you've told me now, so many stories of 'Tina' - and how you'd play with her in your back yard - throw the ball, take her for walks - spend the quiet time in the evening - drinking your beer, smoking a cigarette… you've mentioned how you'd stroke her fur, and I'm willing to bet – you would even sit and hold her hand" as he smiled…

In that moment, I pictured her lying on her back - paws in the air - reaching for my hand. That ball clenched in her mouth, her tongue hanging out, and a smile shining in her eyes… as Father John continued:

"Jack - she wasn't just a dog - she was your partner on, and off duty… she comforted you, and she saved you… even though she sacrificed herself for you - and you feel the loss… think about the times you just sat with her…"

For a moment I may have even smiled. For a moment I may have even felt a sense of joy. Then, the thoughts of her not being here brought back the pain... I could hear father John as he was still talking...

As I listened I felt my throat tighten. "She wasn't just a dog," I muttered, barely above a whisper. Father John nodded. "No, she was more than that. She was your companion - your partner in every sense. When the world felt like it was in chaos, she was there. She protected you. She understood you in a way that no one else could. And even though she's gone, Jack, those moments still belong to you."

I looked down at my hands, at Father John's grip. His words were starting to break through. "Sometimes I still feel her there, like she's sitting beside me," I said, my voice cracking. "But when I remember those good moments, it's like it just brings all the pain back."

Father John squeezed my hands gently, grounding me. "That's because love and loss are intertwined. But you can choose what to focus on, Jack. You can choose to honor those moments with Tina - the times she brought you peace, not the pain of her loss. She gave her life for you because that's who she was. She wanted you to live, to be here in this moment. Jack — healing, it's all in your hands."

The memories of that night in the alley flooded back - gunshots, and the look in her eyes as they drifted away across the rainbow bridge. She lay in my arms. I could feel her fur, her blood, the slow rhythm of her breathing... the sights — the sounds, and even the smell - all of it, right there, in my mind, and in my hands. I remembered my own pain - the radio calls, the ambulance - and then the bright lights of the hospital, where the confusion turned into a thick fog. I remember waking up after surgery, but it didn't feel like waking at all.

I remember the grip of my wife's hands on mine - almost as if I could barely feel them, yet they held me tight. The sounds of the machines keeping me alive... I wasn't holding onto memories anymore. I was holding onto life. The life my partner saved. The life my wife saved - and wanted me to keep. In that moment, it was all in my hands.

My breath caught as the memories gripped me, so vivid, so raw that they might as well have been happening again. The alley. The gunshots. Tina's eyes locking with mine as her strength faded - her look drifting away like a shadow into the dusk. Her last gift to me was her life.

Still sitting across from Father John, I closed my eyes. In my mind, I heard the faint echo of the hospital room - the cold, sterile beeping of the machines that kept me breathing. I wasn't awake, not fully. But I remember her hands - my wife's hands. Gripping mine as if she was holding me to this world. Her silent plea, begging me to fight, to stay. To live.

"I wasn't just holding on to memories," I murmured, barely recognizing my own voice. "I was holding onto life. The life Tina gave me. The life my wife wanted me to keep... It was all in my hands."

Father John remained quiet, letting the weight of my words hang between us. I could feel his presence - steady and warm - grounding me like the earth beneath my feet.

"You're right, Jack," he finally said. "It was in your hands. But you weren't alone. Your wife, even Tina in a way - they were there, holding you, carrying you when you couldn't carry yourself. And now, it's up to you to keep holding on. To honor them by choosing the path to heal."

Father John knew what I was going through - I remembered what he told me - what he went through in Viet Nam... he lost a partner - he lost a childhood friend - he knew what it was like - to have someone literally hold them onto life... at the expense of their own...

Father John held my gaze, and I saw something in his eyes - a reflection of my own pain. It wasn't pity, it was recognition. He didn't say anything right away, but I could tell he was remembering. The lines on his face softened, "I get it, Jack," he finally said, his voice low and steady. "I know you think no one could understand. But _I_ do. I've been where you are." He softly lowered his hand to his chest - as if feeling the pain of his own wounds all over again. "My friend gave me his life, Jack. Just like Tina gave you hers. I've had to live with that... with the weight of it. You're not alone in this,"

Father John said softly. "It's heavy. But you don't have to carry it by yourself."

"He gave me his life, Jack, and I'll carry it with me until the day I die." I swallowed hard, feeling my chest tighten, knowing Father John's story mirrored my own. The look in Father John's eyes seemed to say 'helping you - Jack - is helping me bring closure to my own story.'

My thoughts returned to Tina's sacrifice, and it echoed in my mind - the way she stayed with me until the end, until I was safe. And just like Father John, I would carry her with me forever, her memory woven into every beat of my heart.

Father John continued: his voice now somewhat raw with emotion. "I've made peace with it now. Because my friend didn't save me to live in guilt or regret. He saved me so I could live. He gave me life, and that's what I hold in my hand – so the pain of his loss isn't shadowed by the weight of him not being here…"

We sat in the quiet of the office – two men who have, and are now facing the challenge of grief… working on mending the pain, and growing past the hurt… Father John leaned back in his chair, his eyes fixed on something distant, as if searching for answers in the cracks of the ceiling. "You know, Jack," he said after a long pause, "there's an old line from a poem, from John Greenleaf Whittier that I've always carried with me. 'Of all sad words of tongue and pen, the saddest are... it might have been.'"

I let the words settle, their meaning curling around my thoughts like smoke from a dying fire.

Father John looked back at me, his gaze steady, filled with both sorrow and resolve. "The past is full of those words, isn't it? But here's what I've learned: we can't let the 'might have beens' keep us from the 'what could still be.' Healing... real healing... starts when we let go of what we can't change and choose to step forward, even if it's just one small step at a time. Jack – in this case... one spoke at a time."

For the first time in a long while, his words didn't feel like a platitude. They felt real - earned through pain, struggle, and a journey not unlike my own.

"Jack... Tina didn't give her life just to have you drown in grief. She saved you - so you could keep living… hold her in your hand, see her in your heart – feel her when you're lonely… and accept her sacrifice as a gift of love. Know that when you hold her memory – that she isn't ever far away. Jack – if you can see the light hidden in the shadows of loss, you can feel the peace of what true love is. Love isn't always without pain, but love is knowing sacrifice… and love is a gift that sheds light on the future. And **that** is what you hold in your hand.

"The world around you is like the rim of our wagon wheel, and you can choose which spokes reach you. What you choose is what will bring you joy – or pain… Jack – this is all in your hands."

I couldn't move… I couldn't even breathe at the moment. Father John's words cut me to the quick. I was speechless. Father John went on…

"The day you and Bell spent in the countryside watching the Sheepdogs – you held in your hand a moment of peace while you could think of Tina without the pain. Jack – that is how you have to think about the spokes of the wagon wheel – to find a moment of peace – a light that can erase each shadow of darkness – each spoke of the wheel that wants to hurt you. I can't promise it will be easy, but with each ray of sunshine you can find, the memory of Tina will brighten, and the bond you and Bell have will be even stronger.

**

I walked away from Father John feeling humbled - again. The weight of his words settled into my chest as I rode home in the quiet of the night. The hum of the bike beneath me was steady, almost meditative, but my thoughts were anything but still.

When I pulled into the driveway, the soft glow of the porch light flicked on. I sat there for a moment, just breathing. The night was calm, but inside me, emotions churned - fresh, raw. Slowly, I climbed off the bike, feeling the gravity of the evening in every step as I approached the house.

Before I could reach the door, I heard the familiar sound of the latch turning. The door creaked open, and there she was - my wife. The one who had held me by the hand during the darkest of times. The one who stayed by my side. The one who kept me alive... She was the one who had encouraged me to keep going, even when I felt like I couldn't.

Our eyes met, and in that moment, we didn't need words. We both knew. The loss, the pain - the shared love of someone we both cherished - it all hung in the air between us, unspoken but understood.

She reached out, taking my hand in hers. Her touch was soft, familiar, grounding. We stood there on the threshold, wrapped in a silence that said everything we needed to say. I didn't want the moment to end... I swore to myself I would learn to - I would *force* myself to... cherish every moment with her - forever.

For the first time in a long while, I felt a small sense of peace settle into my heart. My heart that she'd held and protected... and in spite of her own loss... she remained strong... reminding me of the famous words...

"The most beautiful things in life are not seen, but felt by the heart." *Helen Keller*

As I sit on my patio - I can still feel my partner sit with me in the quiet of the evening. I now cherish every moment I thought would never end – even if it is only the memory of every touch of her paw in my hand.

I feel the presence of my wife standing behind me, as she quietly takes a seat beside me… in the silence of the evening we just sit…

And hold hands.

Chapter 9

The Protector of Heroes

They told me once - that I was a hero. I didn't feel like one. I just felt angry. With every step I walk alone - I remember the companion I wish I could have saved.

My mind realizes the logic, but my heart still aches.

Sometimes I sit alone on the patio - I still see the toys she would play with… sometimes I can still hear her steps, and feel her by my side. Bell will talk about the moments she shared with her, and I'm hurt all over again knowing that she feels Tina's loss ever as much - maybe even more… than I do.

I sit and look at pictures in the album - of so many dogs I've served with. Each having their own special memories. From the deserts of Iraq - to the jungles of the city – I always knew I could stare into the eyes of the devil, or face the unknown and know that I was safe…. With them by my side.

I didn't feel much like a hero. I was just doing a job. I was simply lucky enough to be the partner to the real heroes - the dogs that kept me alive. I was the partner that was lucky enough to have served with Tina.

Father John reminds me that the sorrow, the anger, and the guilt may never fully go away. I guess in time I'll learn how to replace these feelings - with joy, with laughter, and maybe even peace.

I can only hope.

**

Father John once asked me "Why do you think losing Tina was harder on you than - let's say - moving on from your other K9 partners, or the many other hard things that haunt you, Jack?"

I fumbled with my words: "I don't... I don't really know... maybe it was the way I lost her, maybe it was the relationship I had with her... I don't really know."

I sat deep in thought - knowing my other K9 partners went to good homes, living comfortably in retirement. Even Gunner was able to come home to live with us after he served.

Maybe it was the years of nightmares and haunting images that had piled up - one on top of the other. In a way, not having a direct or personal connection with the strangers I was sent to protect made it easier - at least sometimes - to detach from the memories… those mental snapshots of everything I'd seen and experienced on the job.

But detachment doesn't mean forgetting. Those memories still waited - tucked away in the corners of my mind - surfacing when I least expected it. Faces I didn't know, cries I couldn't stop, moments I couldn't change… they stayed with me, no matter how far I tried to push them away.

It's hard to say. The only way I could explain it to Father John why losing Tina was so hard - was that, somehow, it all came down to the bond I shared with such a remarkable creature.

"She wasn't just a partner," I said slowly. "She was part of my family. Tina wasn't like the others. Tina had something really special about her. But like the others - she came home with me, slept at my feet, and loved my kids... My wife, well, she looked at Tina like our own – just like Gunner."

Father John gave a knowing nod. "So maybe, for you, it's not just about losing a fellow officer. It's about losing part of your family."

I blinked a few times, not sure how to respond. He was right. It wasn't just the job this time - it was family I couldn't protect.

I wasn't just angry at a man, who shot a dog, I was angry at the man who took a family member...

"My wife keeps her pain quieter than I do. She doesn't say much, but I see it in the way she carefully walks past the empty dog bed or how she keeps some of Tina's old toys tucked away in the drawer we swore we'd clean out months ago, but always knew we never would. It's always little things - like how she still makes the same amount of food for dinner as if Tina were still around for 'her' share...

"Sometimes, I find her sitting on the porch, sipping her coffee, staring at nothing. I know what she's thinking. The silence between us has grown familiar, a kind of shared understanding that words can't seem to touch. We both feel it - this gaping absence Tina left behind. But we're so wrapped in our own ways of coping, it's like we're each carrying the weight - and comforted that we aren't alone.

"Our kids come by more often now, bringing our grandchildren. They've always been close to us, but lately, it feels like they're trying to fill in the gaps Tina left behind. They never say much about it, but I know they feel the loss too. They grew up around the dogs, even pretended to train with them when they were younger. Tina was more than a partner to me - she was part of the family. Father, I know Bell misses Tina, and when she suggested getting another dog, well - I just don't know..."

Father John listened, silent with his understanding way. His gaze direct, but filled with compassion. When he finally spoke, he said softly:

"Jack, bringing another dog into your life doesn't mean you're replacing Tina. It means you're honoring her. It means you're taking all that she taught you - the loyalty, the courage, the bond you shared - and sharing it with another. Tina wouldn't want you to walk this path alone. A new partner doesn't erase the past; it helps you carry it forward. And Jack... both you and Bell – you deserve to keep walking, to keep living, with someone special by your side."

**

One day, my granddaughter Izzy came bounding into the living room, her feet tapping against the hardwood like Tina's paws used to. It was a comforting sound, and I half-expected her to drop a ball at my feet, the way Tina used to do, but instead, she had something behind her back. She stood there, grinning, the way kids do when they're about to reveal a secret they've kept for too long. "Grandpa," she said, her voice full of excitement, "we have a surprise for you."

I looked at my son, who was standing behind her, arms crossed and a knowing smile on his face. He nodded, giving her the go-ahead. Slowly, Izzy pulled out a small framed photo from behind her back. It took me a second to realize what I was looking at - the picture of me with Tina, from our days on the force. Next to it was another photo, one that I hadn't seen before.

It was a picture of a German Shepherd puppy - tiny, with those big upright ears - and bright eyes that seemed to sparkle with energy. At the bottom of the photo, written in bold letters, was the name: *Athena*. I felt my heart catch in my throat. "What is this?" I asked, my voice rougher than I intended.

My son Jason stepped forward. "Dad, we've all been feeling Tina's loss. We know how much she meant to you, and to all of us. Izzy and I... well, we talked with the department and with Mom. We also reached out to the breeder in Germany." He paused, and I could feel the weight of what he was about to say.

"We've raised the money, with the help of the community, your colleagues, and... we've arranged for another Shepherd. **Athena** is from the same parents as Tina. We contacted them, and they remembered Tina, and thought '**Athena**' wouldn't just be the right tribute to her, and being her 'sister' – would continue her legacy." Before my son could finish – my granddaughter Izzy interrupted with a burst of energy "She's waiting for you, grandpa. She's yours if you're ready."

I couldn't speak. The mixture of emotions - grief, hope, guilt - all swirled around me. I looked at my wife, who was watching me carefully, her eyes reflecting her own feelings. For the first time in months, there was something in her expression other than sadness.

"We thought it was time," she said softly. "But it's up to you."

I held the photo of **Athena** in my hands, staring at her curious little face. It was like looking into the future while remembering the past - one filled with both the pain of that past and the possibility of healing. The weight of loss was still there, but for the first time, I felt something else creeping in alongside it.

Maybe Father John was right. Maybe the sorrow and guilt would never fully go away. But maybe, just maybe, there was room for something else - something that Tina would have wanted for me.

"I think… I think it's time," I whispered, my voice breaking.

Jason clapped me on the back, and Izzy threw her arms around my neck. Even my wife smiled her eyes moist with a joy we hadn't been able to find in months.

Athena - named after the goddess of war and protector of heroes - would soon be by my side. But it would be a while before she could come… Not that she would replace Tina, but come to honor her. And maybe, in time, she'd teach *me* how to heal.

**

It wasn't hard for me to figure, I knew something was going on. The surprise from my granddaughter Izzy – of her 'spear-heading' the fundraising - and my family - the police and all - arranging it… I thought that around every turn of the corner – they would try to surprise me.

Yes - I could tell something was going on - even Father John was 'tight-lipped' about it all. I had been to a few of the department "events" - expecting something - but it all ended up being all the usual stuff - friends retiring - dedicating new equipment and technology - the "smoke-screens" I thought would be their surprise... yes... I kept waiting.

I was sitting on my patio - the morning coffee, the lonely memories of Tina. I could hardly bring myself to move - or put the toys away. In some ways I thought it would betray our last moments in the back yard together. Something I didn't want to - or couldn't bring myself to do.

My dear wife... Bell could tell I was feeling a bit nostalgic, and she suggested we go out for a bit of brunch at our little café we all know and like. It's the same place where I like to meet my biker friends.

I suggested we ride down on the bike, but she said "she wasn't in the mood" to ride the bike, so we hopped in the truck, and drove the few miles down through the neighborhood - a nice day, and not a lot of traffic. I thought it would have been a perfect day for the bike... As I pulled into the parking lot - I could see a lot of the big motorcycles of some of my friends from "group", and a couple of police cars. "Nothing out of the usual" I thought...

My wife and I walked into the café and we were greeted by the staff that we've come to know - big smiles on their faces. I should have known something was up. What I didn't see - were the cars of all my kids hidden behind the building...

We were escorted to the back room of the seating area where they could accommodate large groups - parties and such - where we were greeted again by... a lot of my cop friends, biker friends, Father John - my kids and grandkids... and breaking through the group was my oldest granddaughter Izzy with a beautiful little girl...

She couldn't hold back her excitement, and for nearly a half of a heartbeat - I thought "**Tina**?"

This beautiful little girl was nearly a mirror image of my Tina. Born and bred from the same parents. She had the same look in her eyes - bright and beautiful. Izzy let her loose and as if she knew - this little girl came prancing right up to me and my wife.

Nearly everyone present said together: "Jack - meet '**Athena**'!"

I bent down to greet her - and as if it were Tina herself - her mannerisms - her smell… it was as if she was the reincarnation of the savior that pulled me from the line of fire… and sacrificed herself for me.

She leaned into me in such a familiar way, and as if she already knew - the look in her eyes seemed to let me know she could feel the pain - the loss… the memories…

I whispered softly in her ear - *"You have some pretty big shoes to fill, little girl"* - and she tilted her head ever so slightly the way German Shepherds do, and she looked deep into my eyes. In that silent exchange, it was as if she was saying, *"I know, and I'm here. I'll do my best for you."* Her gaze was steady, full of warmth, trust, and an unspoken promise, as if she understood the weight of what she was stepping into. Her youth never hindered her brightness; her love was truly a comfort…

It seemed like a celebration for newness, and **Athena** never strayed from my wife and me. There was something so familiar about her - something we've missed. Father John simply smiled.

**

We walked Athena out to where we were parked. She seemed to know what to do when I let her off from her leash and nosed at the handle as if she tried to open the door to my truck… She hopped into the driver seat - proud and perky - and looked at me as if she wanted to drive… I remembered the day I first met Tina… how this was also a near mirror image of - not only what I saw, but what I felt as if **Tina** were still here with me.

I looked at her - smiled… and told her *"Don't you think I'd better drive…"* My wife chuckled, and Athena was more than happy to share the passenger seat with my wife as we drove home. I looked over at Bell, and I chuckled… "So that's why you 'weren't in the mood' to ride the bike down here."

My wife just smiled at me.

Athena seemed relaxed on the short ride home - her typical German Shepherd nose as active as ever. She is big enough that she could sit comfortably, and still see out the windows -

taking in all the sights along the way. I think she could tell she would be loved.

As we got out of the truck - she hopped out and stretched again. We unlatched the front door, and she walked right in. She didn't seem to have a nervous bone in her body. She is curious, alert, and yet comfortable.

We all walked out into the back yard - onto the large patio, and I stopped for a minute - looking at Tina's old toys - the ones we didn't want to move in hopes we would remember our last moments - forever. Athena walked around - and sniffed each of them, and we looked at each other in surprise that she didn't touch them… until…

Athena walked up to one of Tina's old tennis balls - stopped and looked at us… I told her - *"it's Ok girl - I think Tina would be proud to share with you."* Athena carefully picked it up walked over to where we now sat, and placed the ball in my lap… she looked at me as if to ask permission.

We sat there for a few moments - once again in near reverence, the three of us... as if we all could remember - the little girl that brought us all together... the one who saved my life.

Tina

Chapter 10

Moving Forward

Father John's office has become a place of comfort - a place of solace, where the surroundings invite a sense of hope. "I'm still angry," I admitted, though the words felt different this time. Less sharp, maybe. More tired.

Father John nodded, always the patient listener. "Anger has its place, Jack. But it's how we carry it that matters. We can let it eat at us, or we can find a way to let it be a part of our healing."

I stared at the window, watching a bird land on the sill. "And how do I do that?" He smiled, knowing the answer wasn't a simple one. "You've already begun, Jack. You just don't see it yet."

"I feel like I failed" shaking my head – "I let her down Father, I still feel like I let my team down!"

"Jack, you were the supervisor, and you took the lead. You took control, and protected your team, and took two dangerous fugitives into custody.

You were there to make sure those two didn't hurt anyone else, and Tina paid the price for it. Jack, you don't need to keep reliving the pain, you already paid a heavy price. You were shot, and you lost your partner. What more can you expect? You *can* expect to live in peace knowing you and Tina did what you were supposed to do.

"You Jack, didn't stand behind anyone – you were in the lead. You didn't ask anyone to do what you weren't willing to do yourself. You knew the risks, and you did it anyway. Even when you were hit – you didn't stop. You kept firing at the suspect. Through the hail of gunfire Tina was there to drag you to safety. Tina died protecting you, as you were protecting your team."

Father John continued: "you have made so much progress and done wonderfully about replacing harmful emotions with good ones."

I hadn't realized - maybe I **was** healing. Father John's words and lessons not only made sense, but made a difference. The triggers that once haunted me seemed less daunting. It wasn't yet peace, but it was a start.

I rode home deep in my thoughts, hopeful - yet confused. I felt pride in how far I've come, but a little sad that I haven't recognized the pain my wife was going through. So I decided - this is all about to change.

**

My wife and I sat down for coffee with the familiar faces of my biker-cop friends. There was always laughter with this crew, and today was no different. They still got a kick out of calling me **"Preacher,"** a nickname that seemed to have stuck like glue.

"I spoke in a church *'one-time'* - and now look at what I'm stuck with!" I chuckled, shaking my head. "Careful," one of them teased, grinning at my wife. "We might see him up there again someday."

The banter flowed easily, and I found myself relaxing more than I had in months. My wife joined in too, laughing along. It was good to see her smiling again. After a while, the conversation shifted. One of the guys leaned over, looking at me with a smirk. "So, Jack, how's it going with your new girl, **Athena**?"

My wife and I exchanged a glance, her eyes twinkling. "She's a smart one, that's for sure," I said, pride slipping into my voice. "Already reminds me so much of Tina."

"Yeah, we've heard she's sharp. And I'll tell you what - if she's anything like your old girl, we could use her in the field." He paused, letting the idea settle. "Why don't you bring her down? We've got some tracking drills lined up. See how she handles herself." Another one of my friends gave me a gentle look and said: "we really miss your experience too Jack."

I looked at my wife, expecting hesitation, but instead, she smiled. "Why not? It could be fun." I wasn't sure who was more surprised - me or the guys. "You're coming too?"

"Of course," she said her smile widening. "I want to see what all the fuss is about with Athena. Besides," she added with a wink, "it'll be good for both of us."

Soon after, we were getting Athena ready for the training field. As my wife and I stepped outside, Athena bounded toward the truck, her ears alert and her tail sweeping. Her energy was contagious, and I couldn't help but grin. Watching her, I was struck by how much this moment reminded me of the old days - preparing Tina for a day in the field. But this wasn't the past; it was something new. As I opened the truck door and Athena leapt in with eager confidence, I realized this wasn't just about her proving herself. It was about all of us - me, my wife, and Athena - stepping into a new chapter together.

As we pulled up to the training field, our friends were already there, running drills with their dogs. I could see the seriousness in their eyes, but there was also a camaraderie that put me at ease. This wasn't just a job - it was something we all loved. Athena was alert but calm. My wife looked over at me, raising an eyebrow, and then back at Athena "You ready for this?"

One of the guys waved us over, a grin spreading across his face. "There they are! The dynamic duo. Jack, we've got a tracking course set up for you today. Let's see what your girl's got."

I'd already taught Athena to "find your ball" – since she had the habit of losing her ball the way Tina did – and like her sister, had the knack of finding what she wanted... all we had to do now is sharpen what she'd learned.

Athena was already focused, her nose twitching as she took in all the scents. I could tell she was eager to work, and a surge of pride filled my chest. We started with basic commands, and Athena nailed them like she had done it a hundred times. Hans' training in Germany was paying off. But there was something more, and at the moment, I couldn't put 'my finger' on it...

My wife stood beside me, watching with a smile. She had always loved Tina, and seeing her so involved with Athena just felt right. She even called out a few commands herself, and Athena responded without hesitation. Athena seemed be able to anticipate what to do - much like Tina.

The first day went smoothly, better than I expected. Athena impressed everyone with her natural ability, but it wasn't just her instincts - it was her bond with us. That bond, the unspoken connection, I believe... was what made all the difference.

Maybe there was something from beyond - a connection Athena has with Tina... that they were sisters… Athena has a spirit that seemed to ground us - connect us… something special…

**

Over the next few weeks, we settled into a routine. Athena grew sharper with each session, taking on more advanced drills - tracking, detection, even agility. The guys started calling her "the prodigy," half-joking, but I could tell they were impressed. She wasn't just another dog; she had something special, just like Tina before her. We found joy in watching Athena learn and grow, in seeing her step into the role she was meant to fill. The life I thought I left behind didn't seem as heavy as it once was.

One afternoon, after a particularly challenging scent-tracking drill, Athena trotted back toward me with her usual proud strut. "She's incredible," my wife said, shaking her head. "I didn't think it was possible, but she's really living up to Tina's legacy. It's almost surreal that she's so instinctive…"

I nodded, feeling the same. But it wasn't just about living up to Tina - it was about moving forward. About building something new while honoring what we had lost.

**

The field was quiet except for the occasional commands and the steady footfalls of dogs working the course. I watched Athena weave between obstacles, her focus sharp, her body coiled like a spring ready to snap into action at any moment. She had taken to the training like it was second nature, but every time we worked together; I saw the same drive in her eyes - the need to please, to understand, to do the job well. Athena seemed to learn from the others as she was simply watching – as they were performing even more advanced drills in the Schutzhund course…

We had fallen into a rhythm during these sessions. Athena mastered all the drills. It felt good to be out here again, to be part of something bigger than myself. My friends had embraced Athena, my wife, and I, treating us like family, and their dogs had become Athena's playmates.

"She's something special, Jack," one of the guys said as he walked over, tossing a tennis ball in the air for her to catch. She caught it before it hit the ground. We both smiled. "You know, there's a real need for trained dogs. I know she can find anything, and I know she'd even be great at search and rescue, and... You ever thought about putting her in the field?" I blinked, taken aback for a moment. "I don't know... I mean, she's still pretty new to all this."

He smiled. "You'd be surprised how quickly she'll catch on to field work, especially with a nose like hers. We're assisting with some contraband searches in a few days. If you're up for it, we could use an extra set of paws."

I looked at Athena, who had just finished the course and was trotting back and forth waiting to do more. I tossed her ball and she whipped around at full speed to chase it. Her reflexes were lightning fast and she leapt into the air to catch it on a bounce. She was prancing toward us, tongue lolling, but eyes still sharp. I knew *she* was ready.

**

A few days later, we were on our way to meet our friends to do the searches we had arranged, when we got a call to report to the canyon instead. A hiker was missing, and our friends were in need of some real special help. Like Tina before her - Athena seemed to know that there was urgency from the call. I told Bell that I was glad she was going with us – a lost hiker might need medical assistance.

We reported to the campground, and soon we found ourselves getting ready to work. The dense forest undergrowth was thick with the scent of pine and damp earth. It had rained earlier that morning, making the conditions less than ideal for tracking, but I could see Athena's tail wagging, her nose twitching as she caught onto something in the air. The missing person was a local elderly man who was reliant on medication, and had wandered off the trail several days ago. The clock was ticking, and every second mattered.

I crouched down beside Athena, running my hand along her back. *"You ready, girl?"* She looked up at me with those intelligent eyes, as if to say, *I've got this.* I clipped the long leash onto her collar and gave her the command to start searching. Instantly, her demeanor changed - nose to the ground, focused and driven. She looked at me with that look, as if to say "*trust me*." That look! – just like Tina. A narrow sliver of caramel with pupils open wide - blackened to take in every detail… her nose in a near shudder - ears like radar listening… as if she'd done this before. She moved with purpose, zigzagging through the trees, following a scent that was invisible to all of us but vivid to her.

The team followed close behind, watching as Athena led the way. My heart pounded in my chest, a mix of anxiety and pride swirling in my gut. This was it. All the training, all the preparation - it all came down to this moment. Her movements, her strength - all reminded me of that first week with Tina. She reminded me of that lost little boy and how Tina was the hero. As Athena pulled me along - each step was a reminder of the past - as she pulled us into the future. But it was more…

We moved deeper into the forest, the trees closing in around us. I could see Athena picking up speed, her movements more deliberate. She was onto something. I exchanged a glance with my wife, who was walking - even running beside me, her face tense but hopeful.

Minutes passed, feeling like hours, until suddenly, Athena stopped, her body rigid. She let out a sharp bark, like a signal to let us know she found something. My heart leaped as we rushed forward, following her lead.

There, lying among the underbrush, was the missing hiker - alive, but weak. He looked disoriented, but when he saw the team approach, relief washed over his face. Athena sat like she was trained to do when she found something, but eased her way next to him, calm but alert, as if to reassure him that help had arrived.

The rest of the team moved in, Bell checking his vitals and calling for a medical chopper. But I couldn't take my eyes off Athena. She had done it. She had found him. I knelt down beside her, scratching behind her ears. *"Good girl,"* I whispered. *"You did good."*

My wife's training sprang into action, her medical training taking over as she assessed the hiker's condition. "Thank you," he whispered" his voice hoarse. "I didn't think anyone would find me."

"You can thank her," I said, motioning to Athena, who was sitting proudly by his side, her tail thumping against the ground.

My wife still attending to her patient, looked at me, her eyes focused, then she looked at Athena. "She's amazing," she said softly. I nodded, the weight of the moment settling in. This wasn't just about the training anymore. Athena had become more than just a companion - she was a partner, a lifeline for someone in need. And in a way, she was helping me find my own path forward, one prancing step at a time.

We stood in silence for a moment, letting the weight of what had just happened sink in. The hiker was in good hands now, the helicopter lifting him away to the hospital. Athena had not only stepped into Tina's shoes - guiding us both through this journey of healing, but - she commanded the scene. As if somehow connecting with the past, she made the future her own.

My wife rested her hand on my shoulder, her voice barely a whisper. "She's more than just a dog, Jack. She's part of our family." I nodded, swallowing the lump in my throat. "Yeah, she is."

The woods were quiet again, the urgency of the search fading into the background. But inside, I knew something had changed. Not just with Athena, but with me. The anger that had simmered inside me for so long was still there, but it no longer controlled me. There was room for something else now - hope, pride, maybe even peace.

As we made our way back to the truck, Athena trotted faithfully by our side. I glanced at my wife and couldn't help but smile. Our girl hadn't just found a lost stranger today - she'd uncovered something for me, too. Maybe she understood what I didn't yet realize: that maybe I had something more to give.

Maybe I have a purpose waiting - if I was ready to reach for it. Perhaps Tina, in her own way, had brought me Athena to help guide me through the healing. And as we walked down that mountainside together, it was clear…

We were all finally moving forward, together.

**

That night, as Bell and I sat on the patio, Athena sprawled at our feet; I couldn't help but feel a shift within me. The pain of the past was still there, but it was no longer the only thing I carried. In its place was something new - hope, pride, and a renewed sense of purpose.

Bell reached over, resting her hand on mine. "I'm proud of you" she said softly. "We did good," I said, looking down at Athena, who lifted her head at the sound of my voice. "All of us."

As the stars began to dot the night sky, I thought about Father John's words. Maybe I was healing after all. And maybe, just maybe, moving forward didn't mean leaving the past behind. It meant carrying it with me, but in a way that allowed me to keep walking, step by step, toward something better.

I looked down at Athena still resting at our feet… I smiled. I looked toward the heavens, as if to see my Tina, and silently said…

Thank You

Chapter 11

Echoes of the Past

Athena and I started working with the department more and more. It was becoming a great part-time job. The department still recognized my law enforcement certification... and Bell was concerned that it could turn into something more. I assured her it wouldn't. But even as I said it, I knew she could see the weight I carried - those old shadows that followed me every time I put the badge back on, even part-time.

"I think about the night Tina was killed... every day - the bullets that almost took me out too. I know you're worried." Bell nodded slowly, with understanding. "Just promise me you'll talk to me. If it ever gets too much, if the past starts creeping up again... we'll face it together."

**

Bell was working a late shift, and 'we' had nowhere to go for the evening. Athena and I played ball for a while, ate some dinner, and then went to the living room to relax. I picked up an old photo album and sat on the sofa; Athena sat at my feet and rested her chin on my knee. I began to look at the echoes of my past. The pictures that captured moments in time – memories of a lifetime ago that somehow seemed like yesterday.

I flipped through the pages, smiling as I recalled the many days of training in the military. I looked at pictures from my basic training graduation, and then the photos from K-9 training. I met Gunner as a pup at Lackland Air Force Base in Texas. We did our advanced training at the 341st Training Squadron at Joint Base San Antonio, where all military working dogs are bred and trained. It was also where K9 handlers, like me, were taught how to become trainers. Afterward, we went to the 141st Training Center to complete our training, focusing on even more specific skills to prepare us. I told Athena that Gunner used to be my partner, just as she is now.

More pages filled with memories of the dust, dirt, and heat, and the love I'd found amid the chaos of a combat zone. Pictures of Gunner and me, and I chuckled at the snapshot showing us standing in front of our tent – where my friend Wade (Sgt. Callahan to some) made a funny sign that said "Dog House."

I showed Athena so she could see the picture of Bell, Gunner, Sgt. 'Wade' and me, all in our Army clothes. As *if* she could truly understand. She seemed interested for only a moment, and then placed her chin back on my knee.

I sat in the quiet as my mind returned to the adventure, to the sights and sounds – the smells of the camp. I sat thinking and remembering. I could almost smell the dank canvas, and hear far off shells exploding. The sounds of the soldiers clanking their gear, and I could almost feel again where the straps of my pack would leave their mark after a long day on patrol.

I looked at the pictures of me and Gunner, and then looked down at Athena thinking "These two are so similar, and yet so different." He was so large and muscular, and she is so slender and sleek. I told Athena *"I loved, and still love every one of you"* as my hand left holding the page for a moment to stroke her fur. The motion brought back memories like I could feel Gunner's fur again, as I would remove his gear, and the

familiar damp scent of dog filled my mind –
recalling the times I would 'sneak' him into the
outdoor canvas showers with me. Athena sensing
my nostalgia moved to sit on the sofa with me,
and now rested her head on my lap.

My mind raced back to Gunner and how every
patrol, and every mission I'd worry about
keeping him safe, but I did. Whenever he would
'indicate' the presence of a bomb or an explosive
I'd pull him back so he wouldn't set off an
explosion. We'd mark the location so the
"Explosive Ordinance Disposal" team could
remove them. Day after day we'd walk the paths
of danger, and we learned to trust each other like
no other.

I remembered the day on patrol. Gunner had
detected a number of explosives and we'd
flagged each of them so the EOD team could
dispose of them.

One of the 'flags' must have blown away in the
breeze, and left an anti-personnel bomb
undetected. The ordinance disposal team was in
danger. Gunner and I were "standing by" to
confirm the explosives in the area were in fact
clear for troop movement. Sgt. Callahan – Wade

– was approaching one of the other 'flags' and before he could reach that threat – Gunner broke free from my hold and lunged toward Wade. In a leap, Gunner tackled Wade and pushed him away from the undetected bomb that was buried beneath the ground. Gunner immediately pointed toward the hidden explosive "on point" and wouldn't release his warning until we 'flagged' the threat – as he'd been trained. My friend – Wade... never forgot that. Gunner truly saved his life that day.

I thumbed through the pages and smiled at the photos of Bell and Gunner together – both smiling. It brought back so many good memories. I tried to focus on the happy moments from way back then - maybe in a way to help, so I could focus on the happy memories with Tina.

I remembered the day Gunner and I met Bell at the hospital and how she immediately fell in love with him too. How the three of us became so close. The three of us were almost like a family.

I closed the album and thought back about how hard it was when our time in the combat zone was coming to a close. I petitioned the Air Force to adopt Gunner, and my Attempts fell on deaf ears. Both Bell and I wrote letters explaining that Gunner wasn't just 'surplus' equipment to be disposed of when his service came to a close... that Gunner deserved to be treated like a true Veteran, and treated with respect... but still... our plea went nowhere.

Bell and I would stay up late at night writing letters – we called our families back home – and we all started a campaign to save Gunner. **Wade** even began a letter writing campaign to save the one who saved him – telling the story of a true hero – a true soldier who risked his life to save his own.

It wasn't until Bell and I both petitioned our Senator from back home – Jake Garn, a US Navy hero and the first sitting Senator who became an Astronaut... Bell and I were sure that if anyone could save Gunner – he could. We both knew that we were Gunner's only chance to live. K-9 Veterans were destroyed after service, and I couldn't bear the thought of him being 'put to sleep' after he'd saved so many lives – finding so many bombs.

Gunner was my partner in service – he was my friend, he was my family, and became a living symbol of Bell's and my bond in a war zone. We had to save him. Gunner was a life worth saving… and we were determined to save him. But time was running out. Both Bell and I received our transfer letters to go home… Gunner didn't.

Two days before we were to leave the camp and return to the States, my company's administrative clerk called me in to receive a phone call. He motioned for me to pick up the phone, and I said 'hello.' I was prepared to hear the worst. I was prepared for the news that Gunner would be 'put down' as surplus equipment. My heart was in my gut, and my mind was a blur of heartbreak. I remember the despair. I remember the hurt.

The voice on the other end announced himself as Senator Garn from Utah – I was speechless. All I could say (again) was 'hello' not knowing what to expect next.

The conversation was short. He said within hours we would have Gunner's transfer orders, and that he was proud to inform us we would be allowed to adopt our companion. I didn't know what to say – I could barely muster the words –"Thank

You Senator" my voice was thick with emotion, or maybe it was choked by the 'dust' in the air…

As I reminisced - I looked deep into Athena eyes as if I remember looking into Gunners – or even Tina's eyes. I was thinking – then saying… *"You know girl – there isn't anything I wouldn't do for you – either…"*

I remember after receiving that phone call from the Senator, that I immediately ran to let Bell know – I ran into my tent and found her with Gunner. She could tell by the look in my eyes I had good news. I didn't have to say a word…

"So we get to keep him?" she said, almost laughing. I could only nod. We both hugged him tightly - we couldn't let him go. He was coming home with us. Gunner was no longer just a war hero or a K-9 partner. He was ours, and we were his.

We called everyone so we could to give them the good news. The next couple of days were a blur of excitement and anticipation. We were **finally** going home. **All of us**.

We arrived at the Air Force Base in Utah met by so many of the friends and family that helped in our letter writing campaign, and Gunner took it all in, amid all the hugs and congratulations.

**

Later that week, I sat with Father John and shared stories of Gunner – the celebration at the base and how Gunner helped both Bell and me transition to civilian life. We chuckled at his constant sniffing – always on the lookout, ever the soldier, trained to protect us. We reminisced, and I told Father John that Gunner lived another nine years, healthy and happy.

As I transitioned to working with dogs on the Force, for a while we had two German Shepherds, and it was almost like Gunner had helped train my new duty partner, Shadow. I loved how they got along. Our work to save K-9 heroes gave me a deep sense of purpose. We kept writing letters, and seven years after we saved Gunner, our efforts – along with the efforts of countless others – culminated in the passage of Public Law 106-446 (10 U.S.C. 2583), better known as "Robby's Law," enacted in the fall of 2000. This law prioritized former handlers for the adoption of their K-9 partners and, finally, recognized the unique bond that forms between them during service.

Our chat stirred something deeper within me. Father John must have seen it in my eyes as we talked. His expression softened, solemn but kind. "Jack," he said, his voice steady and understanding, "maybe that's why losing Tina was so hard? You fought so hard to save Gunner, but you couldn't save her?"

Father John's questions lingered in my thoughts, but there was a small smile growing inside me - in the memory that came next. One time, my old Army friend Wade, who'd joined the County Sheriff's Department, stopped by our house on his way to the department's office – so he could pick up some evidence bags I had for him. As he came in, I thought Gunner might have remembered him, but when Wade walked through the door, Gunner started sniffing him all around and then sat. Wade looked at me, and I smiled. "You've got something on you, don't you?" I said.

Wade grinned back, reached into his pocket, and pulled out a bag of cocaine he'd been carrying to 'book' into evidence. We all laughed, but Gunner? He just thought he was doing his job.

I sat in silence for a moment – with the fond memory, but then his words hit me as I thought of Tina, and, I hesitated – knowing I'd said those words before – now it became a reality. I didn't know what to say… "Maybe," I finally admitted, my voice barely above a whisper. "Maybe that's why losing Tina - maybe that's why it's been so hard."

As we talked, I sat in reflection, the deep pain from Tina's death lingered like an open wound that would heal slowly. Physically healed, yes, but there was a gaping void inside that no search mission or rescue operation could fill.

I realized that part of my need to return to the field was a way of facing my fears - the fear of losing control again, the fear of feeling helpless like I did that night. Every time I donned the uniform or took Athena out for a search, it felt like I was daring myself to step closer to that edge.

**

One evening - the three of us came home from working at the county fairgrounds. I'd been working security for the rodeo, and Bell was at a "Nursing aid station." It was a long day, and we all grabbed some dinner at a fast-food drive-in on the way home. We settled in for the evening, and sat down on the sofa to watch some television. We were watching the news, and they were showing the people in Florida affected by a hurricane. I'd mentioned to "my girls" that I was glad we don't get those kinds of storms here in the mountains...

We watched the images of people evacuating, something stirred deep inside me. The chaos, the fear - it was all too familiar.

Shortly after, my wife's phone rang, cutting through the quiet. She stood up, walking a few steps away as she answered it. I could see from the look on her face that it wasn't a social call. I glanced down at Athena, noticing something I hadn't expected. She had lifted her head, ears perked, her eyes focused on Isabel with an intensity that I had learned to trust. Athena knew. Somehow, she knew.

"That was the Red Cross," she said softly. "They're asking if we could assist with the hurricane relief effort in Florida. They know that they'll be overwhelmed, Jack, and... They need people with search and rescue experience."

For a moment, I didn't say anything. Athena stood up, coming to my side as if she understood that her time had come again. I ran my hand over her fur, feeling the strength she carried. Bell watched us both, waiting.

"Looks like we're needed," I finally said, meeting her gaze. "All of us." Looking down at Athena, I could feel her anticipation. She knew something was coming, something bigger. It was as if her own instincts were guiding her - like she was ready to face whatever we'd find. I smiled, grateful for her strength, and for the silent bond that connected us all. "Together," I agreed. "We'll face it together."

Athena watched intently as we began to pack our bags, then turned around and ran out of the room. It wasn't but a few moments when - she proudly pranced back in dragging her leash and harness - with a 'cheesy' smile... I chuckled and thought - yes - she knows, she always seems to know.

**

The next morning, we loaded the truck with everything we'd need for the long trip. Athena could tell there was an excitement in the 'air' - and of course, she loves going for rides in the truck. We were told the hurricane would likely have weakened by the time we arrived - but that's when the real work would start.

We had to wait at the Red Cross camp in Alabama while the Interstate 10 could be cleared. FEMA officials said they were re-assigning us. As soon as the roads opened up we could proceed to Tyndall Air Force Base - where all the K-9 crews would set-up for search and rescue operations. And it didn't take long. The news could hardly describe the devastation and debris that remained even after the winds had died down.

The Air Force Base brought back so many memories of military life. For both of us. These were the echoes from my past I'd thought were long gone. My wife joked around - remembering the military food, but I told her that we'd get used to it again. And we did. Athena didn't seem to mind either. I wasn't sure if I missed this life or if I'd just never fully left it behind.

For days we traveled into the disaster zone by boat - up through the "North Bay" area up into Deer Point Lake. We were surprised at how much flooding there was - it was as if the entire area was a lake. Water had swallowed up whole neighborhoods, turning them into ghostly canals where only rooftops and treetops broke the surface.

Most of our searches merely confirmed that evacuated areas didn't have any remaining people. The days were long though, and the few searches where we did find people – so far had happy endings - no serious injuries. It seemed everyone we met enjoyed meeting Athena.

At evening 'chow' we were told they had reports of heavy damage and possible casualties up in the Wausau area - about 40 miles north of the Base. They needed a crew to investigate, but there wouldn't be any open roads. They requested that anyone experienced with "aerial" travel and K-9 searches report to the communications tent. Before I knew it - my wife was there volunteering us for the job. She told them that she used to be an Army nurse, and part of the current K-9 rescue team. They were happy to have us on board. Athena could tell she was about to embark on a new adventure - her eyes sparkled with that familiar gleam. She knew this was her moment, her mission. As we packed up, I could feel it too…

This was why we were here.

Chapter 12

Healing By Helping

The following morning at the base brought the renewed sense of urgency. Reports were finally streaming in with the numbers of people still unaccounted for. We could hardly eat our breakfast - I was slightly apprehensive since it had been a long time since I'd been aboard a helicopter. Athena had never been aboard one.

We were told we'd have to fly in since there was too much debris along the waterways further north, and we'd have to land in one of the few 'dry' areas around Wausau. A military van drove us out to the helicopter pads, Athena hopped out ahead of us and sat proudly as we got out and began to don all of our gear. She smiled her big grin as I clicked her leash onto her, and she immediately took the *"on-me"* position and *"heeled"* at my left side as the three of us walked toward the 'chopper' we were assigned to.

It all came back to me as I heard the winding-up of the engines, and the rush of the blades - Athena took it all in - in stride. She jumped a little when we lifted off, but smiled again when she saw us smiling back at her.

The 20 minute flight went quickly, and the pilot began to circle an area he was supposed to land. He kept looking for an open area that wasn't flooded with water. He shouted back at us and told us the only dry area was in the trees, and that we'd have to be lowered down since he couldn't land. I had to think for a minute. We didn't bring a harness for Athena that would let us lower her down. So I thought...

"If the tool 'ain't' right - the man ain't bright" as I remembered the saying from a neighbor - one of the old farmers where I grew up... I asked one of the crew members for some of the carabiner clips they had, and some spare nylon webbing material. I fashioned a harness - threading the webbing through Athena's protective vest. All the training and experience came back and I began to secure Athena to my rescue gear.

I told Bell that I'd go down first - then I asked the chopper crew if they would make sure she was safe and secure. I knew they would, but it made me feel better to ask... We were attached to the cable to let us down, I grabbed onto Athena tightly and said *"OK girl - you ready*!"

We swung out of the door into the blast of air from the chopper blades. I chuckled as the rushing air flapped Athena's chops back and forth. It was hard to tell if she was smiling, or not. The look in her eyes clearly showed that… she was.

We were lowered down through the trees slowly - the one hundred foot drop seemed slow, and the branches of the trees were bending and swaying in the gusts of the powerful rotors, and kept hitting at us as if trying to keep us away…

I felt the earth under foot, and the slack in the cable, and used the radio to let them know we were on the ground. I quickly released the rigging, and told them we were free from the cable. As I was undoing the makeshift harness I'd made for Athena, a man rushed up to us. It looked like he'd been through hell. He was ragged, bruised and bloodied, but told us the real injuries were nearby in a storage shack they'd taken shelter in.

I radioed back to the hovering chopper that my wife needed to bring her advanced medical bag, and I asked the man if he knew of any more people in the area that could be missing. He said he didn't know, but - probably, a lot of people could still be missing.

As Bell was being lowered down Athena took refuge near the base of a large tree, and as soon as the cable went slack again, I immediately unhooked my wife, and the three of us followed the man back to the shack. I told the chopper we were all safe on the ground, and that we would apprise them of the injuries…

It all went quiet for a moment as soon as the helicopter headed back to the base. We opened the door to the shack and there were several people with broken bones, a compound fracture, and lots of deep cuts and bruises. Bell used her radio to apprise the hospital on the base of the patient's conditions, and she began to treat the victims. She told me I should begin to search for any others.

Athena and I began to look through the many damaged buildings. I had to take her off of her leash to prevent it from snagging onto the many branches of broken trees in the debris. She kept looking - sniffing the air for clues. She could get into the areas I couldn't, and would return without indicating the presence of any people. Over and over - she would pause, lift her head, she'd check the ground - and as she was following the unseen path of scent - she would turn back toward me to make sure I was behind her. It wasn't easy - I did my best to keep up.

We would mark each place - to let others know we'd already confirmed there were no casualties in that building...

House after house - sloshing through mud and swampy water, she never backed off from searching. She was relentless. She began to push through into an area that soon got too deep for her to walk. I bent down, and placed her on my shoulders, and then we proceeded to wade into an area she seemed to get excited for. The depth of the water was nearly up to my chest, but we kept walking. As soon as I could let her down back to the ground, she began to run toward another broken house... meanwhile, in the distance now - I could hear the repeated arrivals and departures of the helicopters attending to the others where my wife was treating the injured.

Athena pushed ahead through the twisted mess of broken boards and debris, her nose low to the ground, tail held high, every step calculated and focused. I stayed close behind, watching her ears twitch and her head tilt as she assessed each new scent and sound.

At one point, Athena stopped, lifted her head and sniffed the air with intensity. Without hesitation, she glanced back at me, as if to say, *"This way."* I nodded, trusting her instincts, and followed as she forged a path through the wreckage. Despite the mud and the risk of sharp debris, she pressed forward, unwavering, guiding me to what lay hidden ahead. It was clear her determination was as fierce as mine, if not more so.

Athena tried to get into a heavily damaged house, but couldn't. She indicated that she knew someone was inside. I got to the house and started to call out to anyone who could be inside. There was no answer. The doors seemed to be locked. As I looked through windows I thought I could see an individual on the floor. I took a nearby branch, and broke the window so I could crawl through. I did my best to remove as much glass as I could so I wouldn't get cut. The smell of stagnant water - moldy with a hint of wet wood hits me and I can't help but try to clear the smell from my throat as it gagged me a little. I was already waterlogged from wading through the swamp, the humidity after the hurricane, and the late summer heat. It made our physical exertion even worse.

I approached the individual on the floor, and he appeared to be unconscious. I tried to revive him while I radioed my wife for help. Athena was looking through the broken window watching me - she still looked like she was detecting something. I started CPR on the victim - I kept telling the radio that I needed help. Athena finally jumped through the window and began to sniff through the house. I kept working on the victim... I kept thinking - *"come-on dammit - you gotta live!"* I know I'd been in tight spots before, but the weight of the life in my hands made it feel like the first time.

Athena announced with her "I found it" bark that she found something – and she sat like she'd been trained... I knew she found something. I asked *"what is it girl"* and she started barking again. I dialed "911" on my cell phone and placed it on the ground so the dispatch could zero-in on my location, and as I kept working on the unconscious man - I would tell the voice on the other end what was going on.

In the distance I could hear the sound of another chopper, and hoped it was headed my way… it was. It wasn't long before another rescuer came through the window and took over CPR. I was exhausted, but I rushed to where Athena was on 'point' and I broke through another door, and found a couple of small kids huddled together.

I asked them if they were hurt, and thankfully they weren't. They said their mommy went to find help for their dad, but hadn't come home yet. They said the storm broke their house and that they couldn't leave the room.

I radioed again: this time for another chopper with a lift gurney, and hopefully it would be a medical helicopter with an advanced trauma crew that would come… I got the children out of the house, and they were comforted by Athena; I told her to keep an eye on the kids while I went in again so we could work on saving the children's dad.

I felt an enormous relief when I could hear the sounds of another flight coming in… we were exhausted. The chopper that arrived was in fact a medical team with advanced training. They lowered the paramedic and then retrieved the kids in the gurney. Athena sat proudly, her fur blowing in the rotor gusts, as she watched the kids being lifted into the safety of the helicopter.

By the time the paramedic could transport the dad - there wasn't enough room aboard the next 'rescue-bird' that arrived, since the first 'chopper' had already left with the two children - and so, Athena, the other man who came to help with the rescue, and me - all sat in the quiet while we watched it fly away.

I stood there and watched - opened a little water-proof bag where I had my cigarettes, and lit a smoke. I held the pack in my hand, and tilted it slightly toward my 'new-found' partner, and offered him one… Athena came and leaned up against me and I softly stroked her behind the ear. I told her she was a good girl, and she smiled.

I turned to the man standing to my right, and reached out my hand and said "hi - I'm Jack…it's a pleasure working with you." He shook my hand and said his name was 'Bob', and that he was one of the FEMA volunteers. He said he was an EMT from Las Vegas. I joked with him: "hey - we're nearly neighbors, we're from Utah..."

We sat there in the heat and humidity for a while - joking... about how so many of us came to work together, yet we hardly had the time to get to know each other. For a moment standing with him in the quiet, we laughed together... wondering when they would come back for us...

After what felt like hours, the sound of another chopper's blades broke the stillness. The exhaustion was bone-deep, but there was relief in knowing the kids were safe, the father stabilized, and the storm's aftermath was being handled, piece by piece. We never did hear back on what had happened to the kids' mother.

When our ride finally arrived - I used my makeshift harness for Athena and tied her tight to me. We were lifted the hundred or so feet into the chopper - tired and hungry.

When we got back to the base, my wife was waiting. She was covered in mud, her face a mix of exhaustion and determination. She'd been tending to the injured who had taken shelter in the storage shed, working as tirelessly as we had on the other rescues. "You okay?" she asked, her voice low. I nodded, and for a moment we just stood there, not needing to say anything more.

**

The next few weeks blurred together, filled with more rescues, more broken lives trying to piece themselves together in the aftermath of the hurricane. We pulled people out of flooded homes, patched up the injured, and brought hope where we could. Bell, Athena, and I worked flawlessly together, I couldn't have been more proud.

As things began to quiet down, the weight of it all hit me. I looked at Athena, who was resting at my feet, her job done. Isabel caught my eye, and we shared a tired smile. It wasn't just the hurricane that had battered these people, but life itself. We couldn't fix everything, but for a moment, we were part of something bigger, and that was enough. Although we helped so many shattered lives, I felt a sadness that I never got to know any of the victim's names. This was a time where introductions and pleasantries had no use.

I'm pleased that I could help, and more so that we could be an anonymous force that even for a fleeting moment - touched the lives of strangers.

We had a couple of quiet days at the base - waiting around for any unforeseen reports that hadn't been addressed. Athena was quite the attraction - making friends with all the other K9 teams, rescuers, and even the military personnel... she enjoyed the attention...

Isabel had been in contact with Father John - who had been back at home organizing relief projects through their church. She said he'd been asking about me - and that didn't surprise me at all.

As we packed up to leave - I felt a sense of pride, and yet, a sense of sorrow. I knew we did our best to find everyone - to help everyone we could. I was sad though - that there were some who didn't survive the tempest of the hurricane. Finding and helping victims was rewarding, but locating and recovering those who perished, was always going to be inevitable.

As sad as it is – I'd always known it was going to be a part of the job. Whether an avalanche, an accident, or flood – bringing closure to someone else's loss is always going to be a part of the life I chose. But like the protector – the Sheepdog in me… I'll lick my wounds, and prepare for another day…

Although Tina had been on my mind, and I still missed her - watching Athena work made me feel different. I remembered the words of Father John, and how the sorrow of Tina's loss - and even the anger of losing her, might never go away completely. But through these past few weeks, I started to realize that Father John may have had a point: helping others really did help me…

I can't help but wonder – if that was his plan all along.

Chapter 13

Facing Fear

Like I've said before - unless you have experienced it, you don't know how alive you feel, until you look death in the face.

The life our family has come to know all too well is a life of service to others. It is a life of serving without recognition. It's a life of duty that demands much and often offers little in return. Like the sheepdogs - we serve from a sense of duty... because that's just what we do.

The thin line I have walked a thousand times didn't come from the safety of an office or a routine job, but from stepping into the unknown. I'm driven by a duty that's as much a part of me as breathing. For my family, facing fear isn't a rarity; it's the path we chose, and it's one we walk without applause or reward. It's that moment, standing between chaos and peace, where purpose sharpens, and everything else fades away.

Father John once said that courage - bravery, isn't the absence of being afraid, but being able to conquer it. "It's how you hold your ground - when everything inside you tells you to run."

I'd held onto those words, letting them remind me of why we do this, why we step into the unknown - time and again. For so long now, I have walked in fear. It wasn't the fear for my safety - it was the fear I couldn't save what I loved.

For more than a year now we have been facing the challenges of searching, rescuing, and serving from the shadows - we have done the things that make our world a little safer, and brought people from the depths and darkness of disaster, into the light of hope. But that's just what we do. Athena has risen to every challenge without fear, and I could only hope I would never let her down.

**

Even though we had some down-time at the Air Force base before we came home - we took a few extra days to relax while we unpacked all of our gear. Athena loved the attention we'd been giving her - she really did 'shine' while we were in Florida.

I took Athena with me when I went to meet with Father John, and she greeted him warmly like he was an old friend. We sat in his office and chatted about how good it felt to help, and how I wasn't thinking about the pain - or sorrow, as much as I had been.

We talked about fear… we talked about facing the things that brought us pain… facing the memories that we avoided in order to stay away from hurting. It wasn't easy, but he told me I was ready. "Ready?" I asked… Father John smiled – "yes Jack, you're ready to heal."

When Athena and I walked out to the truck - she hopped in proudly, and looked at me with that funny look as she sat in the driver seat… *"Really little girl"* I chuckled - *"we're going to play this game again: I think maybe I should drive"* as I remembered the way both her and Tina did the first time we met. She hopped again over to the passenger seat… and smiled at me.

I started the truck, and put it into gear. I looked over at her and asked her *"you hungry girl"* - and I swear I could see her nod her head - yes.

We pulled out of the parking lot and drove down the familiar street - approaching the 'burger joint' that Tina loved so much. The place I'd avoided for so long now, because - I was afraid. It was kind of like - being afraid to face the past. I had to tell myself again… "I'm ready to heal."

I slowed the truck - I looked over at Athena, I swallowed hard. But I did it anyway. I pulled into the drive through, and ordered the same things that I used to order for Tina. They gave us our food, and I drove into the same parking spot where Tina and I shared our last meal together. We sat for a few moments in silence, as if Athena knew…

I handed her a burger, and she reached over and snuck a few fries out of the container between us. I couldn't help but see Tina doing this in my mind's eye… watching Athena was almost as if Tina was sitting in here with us - her presence filling the silence in a way I hadn't allowed myself to feel in a long time.

When we got home, I told Bell what we did. She looked proud. She looked at me with kind of a stare, and right when I thought she was about to say something meaningful and profound - she said *"and you didn't bring me anything?"*

We laughed.

As we started back into our routine - Isabel would go to work at the hospital, and I'd take Athena out with the team and work. Bell would go out with us at times - and when we'd get home, we would play in the back yard together… it felt good to laugh again.

**

It wasn't long after that Bell and I had our kids and grandkids over to play in the sprinklers and have a backyard picnic. The summer was nearly over, and we thought it would be a fun day before school started again. Everyone was having a great time. The grandkids were laughing and squealing - splashing through the water, and Athena was running and playing alongside with them. Athena truly was a part of the family. Izzy had a very special connection with Athena - almost as if Athena knew who it was that brought us all together.

We all had fun throughout the morning and into the early afternoon. We ate hotdogs - played games, and had fun throwing the ball for Athena. No one wanted to go home when it was time for grandma Bell to go to work, and for me to take Athena back to the shadows of the city jungle.

My son and granddaughter were the last to leave - they stayed and played with Athena while we got ready. We both came out to the patio where Izzy had dried Athena and brushed her, and made her look pretty. The sunny and clear noon-day sun began to take its occasional cover behind the veil of afternoon clouds. I knelt down and began our routine of fastening the vest and collar - stroking her fur as the shadows of the cloud darkened the afternoon sky for a moment.

I felt a hollow feeling in the pit of my gut. Bell looked at me with a worried look as if some kind of premonition warned her. I continued my routine… as we all began to walk out to the truck, Izzy knelt down by Athena one last time and gave her a hug and said: *"you take care of my grandpa - you pretty little girl."* No sooner than when she said this - a ray of sunshine peered through the clouds, and we all looked at each other with a sense of comfort.

Bell and I drove down to the hospital. I drove up to the ER doors, and kissed her. As she stood up from the passenger side, before she closed the door, she held Athena behind the ears, and then hugged her. I thought I could hear her say, softly under her breath as she held Athena close *"you look after our guy Tina."*

I knew she really said "**Athena**" - but the reality of that instant and the feelings going through me made the moment even more surreal.

**

As we approached the station - we met Stan outside, and began to walk in with him. He said it was probably going to be a slow night, and that they might not need us. We walked into the squad room, and Athena sat down at my feet. We all chatted for a few minutes - drank coffee, and the lieutenant walked in and said they had a 'routine' bomb-threat call, reported to be at a local school. Stan's K9 'Aries' was at the Vet for a cut he'd received, Nick was on vacation, and so - Athena and I were the only K9's on duty that night.

We reported to the school, and walked through every room, passed every locker, and we even patrolled around the entire outer areas… it seemed like we walked for miles… and nothing. She never picked up on anything out of the norm. I knew that even though most of these reports are fake, I wanted to make sure nothing would happen to the school – that there would be nothing dangerous in the building for the upcoming school year. We searched for hours, and I was happy that we found nothing.

When we got to the truck - I let Athena play with her ball for a minute - her 'special' reward for doing a good job. We'd spent most of our shift so far working on clearing the school - so I asked her if she wanted to get some dinner. I knew she wouldn't mind.

Almost, as if testing fate - we ended up at Tina's favorite burger place. We ordered - and Athena barked happily, and we ended up parking in the same usual spot under the evening lights to enjoy our meal. I called Bell at the hospital, and told her that she need not worry, our big 'call' for the night turned out to be nothing. She seemed relieved.

I turned down my radio so we could have a few minutes of quiet while we ate. She ate the burger, and loved 'sneaking' the fries. It was a game she liked to play - even though she truly knew I'd give 'em to her anyway.

Before we finished - like he knew we'd be there… Stan pulled his truck up to mine so our driver windows were next to each other… even though he'd been promoted to Sergeant now - he still addressed *me* as "Sarge." At least it was better than being called… "Preacher."

"You're not going to believe this - Sarge… an inmate at the County Jail slipped away from a highway work crew, and hasn't been seen for hours. The Deputies called for a K9 team to see if we could narrow down the area he might be."

Words cannot describe what went through my mind in those moments - in the words Stan was saying… as if the past came back to haunt me - as if fate was *now* - tempting me…

To face my greatest fears.

We followed Stan to the last known location, the work site on the freeway where the inmate was part of a highway garbage crew. The Deputies from the Jail smiled as we pulled up "we sure are glad to see you two…"

As Athena started sniffing around some of the inmates unwashed clothing the Deputies brought (so Athena could track him) I said *"you guys know what's black and brown, and looks good on prisoners?"* They all just shrugged their shoulders…

I looked at Athena and said… **"German Shepherds"**

They all smiled, some even laughed a little as I tried to lighten the mood, and Athena, well…

She seemed more than excited when I asked her *"you want to find the bad guy."* I put her on the 20 foot lead, and watched her weave back and forth until she honed in on the invisible trail.

It was now quite dark, and I was already a bit tired from our hours of searching at the school, but I knew we were the only way to get a lead on where this guy went. I tried to focus on the task at hand, putting the memories aside. We started out through a wide open alfalfa field, crunching under foot from being nearly dry now at the end of the long summer. In the distance I could see the lights from some farm houses, and from the silhouette of the lights - some fenced off fields where dairy cattle were kept.

I'd learned early in my younger years to watch the animals. Their behavior could reveal more than tracks ever could. As we got closer, the cows' unease was clear - they had bunched up tightly, their usual calm broken. It was a telltale sign, honed by centuries of survival as prey animals. Something wasn't right, and they knew it.

As we approached the barbed wire separating the livestock from the hayfield - I stopped Athena short of her getting tangled in the fence. I reined her in on the long lead, and lifted her carefully so she wouldn't get hurt. I told her to "hold up" while I crossed the fence. But…

Before my feet hit the ground, I slipped. My left leg snagged onto one of the barbs. It slashed through my pant, and cut into my flesh. Athena immediately came to me, as if to attend to my wound. I told her *"it's not bad girl - I'll be all right."* It stung a little, but I knew I could walk on it. I radioed what had happened, and that we were approaching some farm buildings. Athena was on point as she regained the scent trail.

I was happy to see a gate we could go through as we came to the farm compound. I told Athena to heel, and then attached the five foot lead onto her. *"Quiet girl"* I said - *"let's be quiet if we want to find him."* Athena seemed to know exactly what I was saying.

We walked slow, although there was an excitement in Athena's steps - nearly breaking my command to heel. I told the team where we were, and that *'my little girl'* was close to something... my heart was pounding in my chest, and I thought I could hear a little prayer in my heart as I thought - "dear God, please let our back-up get here soon."

We walked closer to the farm buildings - I saw an old Ford pickup, and I nearly panicked as I saw the driver side window was broken out, glass all over the seat and floor; and the empty gun-rack in the back window. That told me everything I needed to know. Yes! I was scared! But I knew that by this time - the fugitive inmate was armed, and that the farmer's family could be in danger.

Athena was leading me toward a barn. An older gentleman poked his head out the door of the farmhouse. I motioned for him to be quiet, and then he pointed toward the old barn. I radioed again - that we have a possible hiding location on the fugitive. I tried to ask quietly if anyone else was here on the farm - he whispered back that he thought his wife was out on the grounds somewhere, but he hadn't seen her for a while. My heart nearly stopped, and I radioed the team we may have a hostage situation… I could hardly hear anything but the pounding of my heart in my ears. But I had to focus. I had to be the force that would protect my little partner… the force that had to come between good… and evil.

I remembered my "combat breathing" - in slow and out slow, and it helped, a little. Athena inching me closer and closer to the barn. I looked down as we walked slowly, and all I could see for a moment was… Tina.

"Focus Jack" I thought to myself: "I'm not going to let this happen… again." I wasn't afraid for myself… I was afraid to lose another partner. My silent thoughts turned into an unspoken prayer: "please God, let her be safe." I watched - and I could tell her ears were zeroing in on something. I said to myself "Focus Jack" as *I* tried to hear what Athena was listening for.

I followed Athena's lead, my grip tightening on her leash as she crept toward the barn door, her muscles coiled. The air was thick with the smell of dust, stale hay, and something else – fear. My hand hovered near my holster as I pushed the barn door open, only to freeze at the sight in front of me.

Through the dimly lit barn I could make-out that the inmate had his arm around the elderly woman, pressing her close in front of him as a human shield. His other hand gripped a shotgun, barrel pointed right at the door. My heart thudded in my chest as his eyes locked onto mine, cold and desperate. I pulled my pistol from the holster holding it at a 'low-ready' – and before I could say anything… the inmate interrupted…

"Drop your gun," he spat, his voice tight with panic. Athena's low growl rumbled at my side, her stance stiff and ready. I didn't move, didn't even blink. "That's not happening," I said calmly, keeping my voice steady, trying to ignore the tremor in my gut.

The woman's eyes were wide, terrified. Athena, sensing the danger, tensed further, her anxious energy making the inmate's hand tremble on the gun. The situation was unraveling fast.

"Back off! Or I swear I'll shoot her!" He tightened his hold, now pressing the muzzle hard into her side. I could feel time slowing down, the echo of Tina's memory still pulling at me. The consequences, the risks - losing another innocent life, another partner - it all rushed through my mind, but I forced myself to focus.

"Athena, easy," I whispered, trying to keep her calm. I needed to buy time, needed him to look anywhere but at the woman. "You don't want to do this," I said, taking slow, deliberate steps closer, hand still steady on my gun. "Let her go. You don't want to make this worse for yourself."

I was scared that I would *do*, or that I would *say* something wrong. I'd never been trained as a hostage negotiator. Athena's focus was intent, and direct. When she saw the inmates grip falter for a fraction of a second, it was all she needed. She sprang forward, lightning fast, slipping past the woman and launching herself straight at him. The woman fell to her knees, crawling away as Athena latched onto the fugitive's arm, her teeth gripping firmly. The shotgun fired, but his aim was wild, missing by inches as Athena's weight brought him down.

I closed the distance in an instant, kicking the gun away as I took hold of his wrists. Athena was holding him in place, her body tense and ready. I was comforted when I heard the sound of the ratchet from the handcuffs.

"*Good girl, Athena*," I breathed, steadying her while securing him. The woman scrambled up, dazed but appeared to be unharmed, and as I glanced back, she met my eyes with a look of silent gratitude. I could finally exhale, the tension in my chest slowly releasing as Athena held her place, unwavering and steadfast now by my side.

I stood quietly for just a moment, gathering my thoughts. Athena remained on point, her eyes locked on the inmate now frozen with fear. I clicked the radio and broke the silence. "We're 10-82," I said - Prisoner in custody.

Cheers broke out over the radio, and I shared directions to our location in the barn, requesting a medical team for the farmer and his wife, and to check for any other injuries.

The inmate started to speak, but I cut him off. "Don't even try," I said. Athena's low, menacing growl kept him silent.

In the distance, I heard the rumble of team vehicles approaching, and only then did I feel a measure of relief settle in.

We could finally breathe easy.

Chapter 14

After the Storm

Deputies from the County Sheriff's office rushed into the barn. I was still at the ready, my gun still drawn, and Athena on point. Her gaze on the inmate locked solid on him and her body tense and set for action. As the Deputies took control of their prisoner, I holstered my pistol, and we exchanged a subtle nod of gratitude as they walked him out to their patrol car. My friend Wade from our Army days – one of the deputies, gave me a pat on the back – and a proud look… that meant more to me than any other look of approval - silent but profound - reminding me that some bonds never fade, even in the line of duty.

Then - for just a moment, Athena and I were alone in the dim light of the barn. I sat down on a bale of hay, and Athena calmly came to my side. I could only think for that moment, as I looked deep into the eyes of this little girl - I was looking into the eyes of Tina. I wiped away only a hint of moisture from my own eyes - stroked her behind the ears and kissed her forehead… all I could whisper to her was…

"You're safe… you're here girl - we made it."

In that moment of silence she rested her head on my knee still looking at me - as if to say *"yes - I'm here, we did it."*

Athena and I gazed into each other's eyes - brief as it was, and her eyes never closed. "Never again" I thought and then I whispered into her ear… *"Never again little girl - I'm never going to lose you."*

**

Athena and I walked out of the barn into a sea of flashing lights. More deputies had arrived by now, and their supervisor came to thank me.

"You're little girl here sure did a fine job! - she sure is well trained for this" he said with pride.

We shook hands, and I smiled back at him saying: "she was trained to track - not for apprehending suspects… but yes, she did really good… she's a natural."

We walked over to the porch of the farmhouse so I could sit for a minute - I could hear the investigators' inside interviewing the farmer and his wife. It was a couple of hours past the time our shift should have ended, and I knew Bell would be worried sick. I reached for my cell phone from my chest pocket, and Athena nosed at it like she knew who I was going to call. I smiled at her and said *"girl - I'm getting too old for this… stuff."* I swear I could hear her laugh.

Bell answered my call, and she was relieved we were ok. Members of my team had already told her what was going on, and that I may be a little detained coming home. I let her know I got cut climbing over a fence, and she asked me if I was ok to drive. I told her I was, but I'd need to find a ride back to our truck. She said Stan was on his way to pick me up.

My wife - always the nurse, told me to meet her at the hospital as soon as I could. Reluctantly… I agreed.

I could see Stan's truck making its way through all the other police vehicles. I chuckled and told Athena - *"look girl, we don't have to walk back through that big field."* She smiled.

Stan hopped out of his truck with a pleased look on his face. I knew by now he'd heard all about what happened in the barn. He blurted out "way to go Sarge" as he clapped me on the back.

Before I could give Athena all the credit - he kneeled down and gave her a big hug - fluffed and scratched her all over and told her how proud of her he is. She loved the attention…

"You got 'em Sarge" Stan said with a grin – *"The two of you sure make an awesome team"*

My heart skipped a beat. He'd said those same words, right before I lost Tina. I knelt down, pulling Athena into another hug. My voice failed me as I struggled for words, and I felt the warmth of her fur against my face, the quiet loyalty that needed no explanation.

"You okay, Sarge?" Stan's voice was soft now, steady.

I managed a half-choked laugh. "Yeah… yeah, I'm fine. Must of been some dust in the air – blew into my eyes, or something."

Stan tilted his head, a gentle, knowing look in his eyes. "Sarge… there's no wind. But it's all right. You're safe here."

I forced a smile, and Athena, as if reading the moment, nuzzled me softly, her eyes holding steady then licking at my face.

Stan reached out his hand and helped me to my feet. We exchanged a look, one of those silent understandings, and then he cracked a smile. "How about we get you back to your truck? Pretty sure Bell's been worried about you." I nodded and looked down at Athena. *"Come on, girl - Uncle Stan's giving us a ride."*

The drive was quiet, the darkened fields slipping past, softened under the dim wash of Stan's dashboard lights. Athena lay at my feet, resting her head on my lap, eyes half-closed in a familiar, shared fatigue. Her steady breathing seemed to mirror the rhythm of the road beneath us. Each time she closed her eyes, I found myself drifting back, seeing that same darkness that had once held Tina.

I wondered if, in some unseen way, Tina was here - allowed, maybe, just this once, to stay close. My thoughts traveled back to the barn, where the shadows and silence had held Athena and me, and somehow, it felt as though the shadows tonight were kinder. In this quiet, I could almost sense Tina alongside us, a reminder of the path that had led me here.

**

After Stan dropped us off at our truck, Athena and I followed him up to the hospital. We pulled up to the hospital entrance, the fluorescent lights casting a soft glow across the lot. Bell was waiting outside, her eyes instantly finding me as we stepped out. The worry melted into a relieved smile, but I could see her nurse instincts kicking in.

"Jack," she sighed, looking at the makeshift bandage on my leg. "And here I thought tonight might be routine for once."

"Guess I keep it interesting, huh?" I grinned, though my voice was softer than usual. Athena leaned in close, her head nudging Bell's leg as if to say, *We're all here.*

Bell laughed and knelt to rub Athena's ears, glancing back up at me. "Looks like *somebody* kept you safe." She stood and, in one quick motion, pulled me into a hug, whispering, "I'm so glad you're all okay."

She stepped back; eyeing my injury with the no-nonsense look that I knew meant I wasn't getting out of here without a check-up. "Alright, tough guy," she said, gesturing towards the ER doors. "Time to patch you up properly."

I smiled a little and said "it's really nothing - just a scratch" and before I could finish Bell piped back: "look here bud – don't you give me any excuses - I'm the one in charge here now." Her warm smile said more than her words, and I couldn't help but chuckle, looking down at Athena, whose tail wagged in agreement. I followed Bell inside, feeling the weight of the day start to lift as the three of us - my wife, my partner, and I - stepped *forward* together.

Bell led me to a treatment room - Athena never leaving my side. She smiled at the two of us "you two - always together." She put me on the treatment bed, and I lowered my hand knowing right where a cold nose and nudging head would be. My wife continued "let's take a look at this leg." She used some scissors to cut open my pant, and was somewhat surprised - "oh my" she said - "you might have to have a couple of stitches."

The ER doctor stopped by, looked at me, nodded his head, turned to my wife and told her "well nurse - I think you can handle this."

"Wait - Doc…" I blurted out, "you're going to let her stitch me up?" he looked at me… and just smiled… and walked out.

Bell left the room for a minute to retrieve the suture kit, and as I lay there on the bed - leg throbbing, my thoughts drifted back to the last time I had to go to the hospital. I was shaken, even haunted, but I was safe… she was safe. I stroked her head remembering the feeling as I stroked Tina… that one last time.

The room was quiet, the smell of antiseptic hanging in the air as I reflected on that night. I hadn't noticed Bell standing in the doorway, allowing me this moment of solitude, as if she could read the thoughts going on in my head.

Bell smiled gently as she knelt beside me, her eyes filled with warmth. "You've come so far, Jack. You're so strong now. I've been thinking about her too."

My wife - my nurse - not only tended to my wounds but more so, cared for my heart. It felt like a reverent moment; the weight of my fears lifted, if only for a breath. Deep within me lay the shadows of sorrow I knew would never fully fade, but with each stitch, I felt my body, and my heart healing. The brightness in Athena's eyes as she gazed at me, glimmered, with a promise of a bright future ahead.

Bell could tell I was exhausted. She knew today hadn't just been about the physical hurdles we'd tackled; she knew I'd finally faced and conquered a fear that had haunted me for so long.

"I bet you two are starving by now," as she chuckled with the warmth of relief in her eyes. "How about we grab a bite?" I knew there wouldn't be any fast-food places open. By now, it had been more than twelve hours since I'd dropped her off for her shift. She had spent a little more than four extra hours at her 2 to 10pm shift at the hospital – and I could tell these were four hours of worry and concern. But Bell had that look. As the lines of worry had slowly changed into relief, she smiled her smile, and said "The kids are back at the house, and they fixed us dinner."

I swung my legs off the treatment bed, ready to stand, only to be met with a wheelchair. I shook my head. "No way I'm riding in that... I'm walking out of here."

"It's hospital policy," another nurse replied with a grin. And despite my protest, I let them wheel me out the doors, Athena never straying far from my side.

At the truck, I reached into my pocket for the keys, only to have Bell take them from me with a knowing smile. "I think I'll drive. You've had a long day," she teased, but I knew her day had been just as long.

Settling into the passenger seat, I felt Athena curl up at my feet, her head resting against my knee. As we drove through the quiet, darkened streets, I gently stroked her, unsnapping her duty gear. Her gaze was steady, a deep satisfaction in her eyes. We shared a long, knowing look; she seemed to sense the memories surfacing in my mind.

"Never again," I whispered to her. *"I'll never leave you. I'll always protect you."* And in that moment, the dust that had blurred my eyes back

at the farm returned. I felt the weight of the day - the closeness of how things could have gone. Without hesitation, this loyal girl had stood *ready to defend me, ready to protect me*, as if it were all that mattered to her. I started to realize in that fleeting moment – that is what Tina wanted too.

And that is what Tina did.

The fear I once felt transformed into pride, swelling inside me. I felt honored, blessed, and incredibly lucky to be loved so deeply by this dog and by so many others in my life. It started to sink in, the risk we all took, the uncertainty we faced every day. We couldn't control everything, even if we wanted to.

Passing the streetlamps that lit the way home seemed to cast away a piece of the fear, the guilt, or maybe even some of the sorrow. Looking down at Athena, I was overcome with a deep love that eased the last of the shadows. I thought of Tina then, and a bittersweet feeling washed over me - honor and pride for her sacrifice, for the protection she had given me.

For the first time in a long time, I felt at peace.

Chapter 15

A Path to The Light

There comes a time in everyone's life, where they have to cross a river. When that time comes - we have to decide whether to cross through the torrent, or find the calm.

My choices were never that clear. I was always forced to cross through the darkness… and violence. It has taken a lifetime for me to find a small token of hope, where I can find a quiet place for me to rest… with a ray of sunshine. But for me it seemed the beams of sunshine were always skirting the clouds – always something more. It was always… something more…

**

Springtime came, and with it, the warmth of pleasant memories. I woke this morning with a nudge from a cold nose - letting me know it was her time to play. She sits quietly as the coffee drips, and then we walk to the patio knowing the world is a safer place as she has become a force that stands between the quiet of the day, and the darkness of the storm.

I sit. I watch. Athena prances up to me and places Tina's ball in my lap. I smile. Athena smiles… and looks at me like *"are you going to throw it - or, what?"*

I feel myself chuckle, and I toss the ball. Reflexes - lightning fast catch and snap - before the ball even reaches the ground. It all comes back to me. The flurry of memories and feelings - the pictures of Athena still vivid in my mind - lightning fast, a leap of faith rescuing a hostage, and apprehending a suspect. The picture in my mind of Tina - choosing to save me. Dragging me through the hail of gunfire… ignoring her injuries - sacrificing herself. For me.

A lifetime of memories - walking through the shadows, always skirting the darkness, the danger, and coming close to death. I sit in the light of springtime remembering the sorrow, the joy, and the thrill of living at the edge. Few can know how alive you are until you come as close to death as we have been.

I couldn't help but chuckle, even with the moisture I held back from my eyes -

remembering the past, and loving the future. Sometimes, tears carry more strength than a thousand unspoken words. For those who've faced life's hardest edges, tears aren't weakness - they're proof of everything we've endured, every loss honored, and every love remembered. They're the tears of quiet moments that remind us we're still human, still connected to the people and memories that shaped us. And maybe, just maybe, letting those tears fall makes room for a little more light.

Over and over I would throw the ball for her, this morning was more than the routine we created… in the cool of this bright morning, it was an epiphany of hope, a beam of sunshine that shed light on a future of healing.

She laid her head on my lap, and I stroked her fur… I looked deep into her eyes and I chuckle *"maybe I am getting too old to keep up like this little girl."* As if my thoughts were swimming through her head, her gaze piercing me - looking as though I were once again comforted by the presence of Tina; it seemed like she was telling me *"it's ok - you've already done so much."*

It was a surreal morning. It was a flash of memories. From living a lifetime at the threshold of survival, to the sight in my mind's eye of a selfless sacrifice; the memories of altruistic love split between the past, and the comfort that was sitting at my feet.

This was a morning I had waited a lifetime for. The thoughts of so many partners, and now - so many retired leashes. Each special creature willing to pay that ultimate price, and the one who ultimately did... I looked up to the sky and tried to see each of their shapes in the clouds. And through a heart healing from all my hurt, and tried to tell them all...

"The honor was mine... I always hoped I was good enough for each of you..."

I don't know if it was closure... I don't know if it was how far I've come to conquering the darkness with a hope of light... but I do know that **I** was the one lucky enough - even blessed... to have been the partner to all of these heroes who protected me.

So, as this past winter has given us time to reflect on the past, spring offers me a light - revealing a new direction. In the quiet of that morning, it was clear: maybe it was time to pass on to others everything these incredible creatures had taught me...

The years of jumping from planes, hard landings in helicopters, the miles of walking - searching for bombs: even the daily life of riding motorcycles, the duty equipment and sitting in police vehicles - it all takes a toll on our bodies. This is something we don't think about when we enlist - or volunteer to serve the public - it just what we do... it's what the Sheepdogs do...

I asked my little girl *"how about we try something a little different... let's go talk to mom..."*

My wife Bell and I talked about slowing things down for us, and maybe start doing something a little different. "What kind of 'different' are you suggesting?" she said with a puzzled look on her face.

"I've been thinking, and I believe we can make an even bigger difference by creating a new division in the department specializing in K9 training. We could even expand it to offer training classes for all the departments - all throughout the state!"

She thought it was a wonderful idea, and we began to come up with a plan. My wife, Stan, Nick, and several other members of the department - well, we all got together, came up with a proposal, and we let my granddaughter Izzy - make the initial pitch to the department, and with our city leaders - with Athena at her side... and they loved it.

Not only did the Chief, and even the Mayor love it, but they suggested we take the plan to the Governor to help with state funding.

At times, it was a whirlwind of activity. We felt a newness of excitement... and maybe even a new sense of purpose. We would be doing the training of the K9's ourselves instead of simply purchasing them - and teaching the officer's how to be handlers – and trainers. My wife and granddaughter rallied support from school kids all over the state, organizing bake sales and art contests to raise awareness for our cause. With the pictures Izzy had taken with Athena, each poster and social media post added a gentle look to the face of public protection. Izzy's passion was infectious, sparking conversations about the vital role K9 units play in our community and reminding everyone of the bond between humans and their canine partners.

At the time of my life I intended to slow things down, well, we were busier than ever. We continued to search, to rescue, and to serve. We did our best to keep up with the demands of duty life, and to keep training new K9 officers, and their human handlers.

The training field we had spent so much time at was busier than ever. The selection process was tough, with each candidate required to prove they could meet the demands of temperament, intelligence, and strength. Opening a training division for K9 officers meant establishing a commitment not just to their duties, but to a lifestyle. Every officer had to be prepared to live with their K9 partner 24/7, understanding that this relationship was built on love, trust, and unwavering loyalty.

Training a K9 was more than teaching a dog to obey commands; it was about fostering a deep connection where teamwork and mutual understanding prevailed. A K9 duo needed to operate as "one," anticipating each other's movements and instincts. Not every officer was cut out for this role; it requires a special temperament, one that could embrace the challenges and joys of sharing their life with a K9 companion. This commitment to serve with a K9 partner is a promise to live with and love your partner. An assurance – a realization even, that you can't just 'put this dog in a cage' like a child would put a toy away on a shelf… this is a life of true partnership.

Similarly, not every dog was destined to become a K9 officer. Only those with the right disposition would make "the cut." Only those who could work seamlessly with other officers and K9 teams, and possessed the innate ability to sense human emotions and detect potential threats – they made the cut. This line of work demanded the proverbial "best of the best," both in human and canine partners.

I found comfort in knowing that my legacy could continue through Athena and the future K9 teams trained in our approach and values. Together, we would cultivate a new generation of dedicated officers and their loyal companions, ensuring that the bond we cherished was passed down and honored for years to come.

Father John came out to watch us during one of our training sessions. Even he stood proud while watching my little protégé, as my Izzy was working on beginning obedience drills with the K9 candidates… and how we were continuing Athena's training to include the "schutzhund" course – since her natural instincts made her perfect for it.

Father John smiled as he watched my granddaughter "She sure takes after her granddad" he said with a slight chuckle - admiring the bond I have with her. I couldn't hold back my pride either: "Yea, but I'm glad she's got her grandmother's looks… I think that balances things out."

"It's inspiring to see the two of you working together like this. It's clear you've made significant progress, Jack."

I nodded my head slowly "Thanks, Father. Some days it feels like a battle, but with Izzy & Bell - and Athena by my side, it's easier to push through."

Father John, with his 'I told you so look' said "The strength of family and companionship is a powerful thing Jack. It reminds me of how we all need a little support in our journeys. You've done so much, and - Jack, you've made great strides in conquering your fear - your guilt. I've noticed that you feel more at peace now... I'm proud of you man, you're learning how to calm your anger by embracing something special."

"I never realized how much I needed that focus, Father - to see the light. Thank you for that. I hadn't understood how much I needed your support until recently. It feels like I'm finally finding my way back from the darkness."

Father John smiled his knowing smile... and said "Yes Jack – and before long... you can be the light for someone else."

I felt a sense of peace – knowing I was finally on a path toward the light.

***

I had just gotten off the phone with my wife. Bell let me know she would be working late. She would be covering part of a shift for a nurse that had 'called-off' sick.

I was on my way to do a routine search at one of the local schools when my cell phone rang again. It was the central dispatch for the State Law

Enforcement system… she asked me to respond to the county just north of ours – to a different school where a suspected cache of unlawful drugs was held. This was a school in an affluent area where a number of the State's political leader's children attended.

I told the dispatcher that I could possibly respond – but she insisted that this was a priority situation – where a judge was already to sign a warrant, but he was reluctant to allow the search unless the best K9 unit would indicate contraband was present. The officers and the judge were hesitant due to the delicate nature – with the possibility of political repercussions if they did a search on one of the children of an important figure of the State.

I told them I would respond. A moment of pride filled my heart knowing that Athena… was considered… one of the best.

I called our dispatch – I informed them I would be doing the scheduled search I was originally assigned to – later. I told them that Salt Lake County needed me to help with something pressing…

I arrived at the High School, and the judge was actually on scene – the officers had the warrant request in hand – the judge ready to sign. I looked at Athena – she looked at me… she had that look, and that drive… I think she actually liked doing… what she was meant to do.

We walked through the halls of the school – not knowing the 'target' area the other officers wanted us to search. Athena stopped by a section of the hallway lockers… and sat.

She pointed her nose toward a single locker, and just sat. The Sergeant radioed out to his team that 'we' got a 'hit' on the locker they'd suspected… the judge signed the warrant, and when they opened the locker… they found a weapon, and a stash of 'drugs.'

We walked out of the school – the officers, and the judge thanked us – that being such a sensitive situation… they needed to be sure of that what they suspected – and that what they were informed of… was in fact… correct.

Athena and I began our drive back south to our home county, and as we were listening to the radio-calls for the area we were passing – we heard something… I wasn't expecting… like I've said… it's always something more. The life I chose rarely gave me – or should I say 'us' – the luxury of knowing what to expect. One moment of duty can change in an instant, and just as the Sheepdog can snap and adjust… so do we.

We heard a call-out on the radio before we reached the narrow stretch of highway where our two counties meet – that the State Prison had an inmate attempting to escape. Athena's ears perked as if she knew what the call meant.

I slowed the truck and hit my emergency lights. I moved the truck over to the right hand lanes and headed off the freeway so we could assist in case there was a need for a search.

We arrived to find the Prison Police units already on site – the inmate caught between the double fence-line. He'd been cut badly by the razor wire, but secured from escaping.

Athena was anxious to help, but by then – there was really nothing we could do to help – other than keep a strong presence for the other inmates in the prison yard.

We stood vigilant watching as the Special Operations extraction team secured the prisoner from within the double fence line. Athena watching everything closely. Officers from the prison housing unit were attempting to clear the recreation yard only to find some of the inmates reluctant to comply.

One by one – the housing officers escorted the crowd in the yard into the doors to the building. We just stood and watched as a number of the men jeered and poked fun at the 'dog-cop' while Athena would growl and attempt to lunge from my hold on her.

The yard was nearly cleared – empty from the group that enjoyed the afternoon sunshine. Athena took particular attention to one… as if she knew.

A straggler – an inmate holding back from going into the building – stood there as if he recognized me. As if he recognized Athena… he stood… he watched… his focus was on me… and Athena.

I couldn't help but wonder why, until it hit me. I looked closer, and I looked again. I looked until I recognized his face… the face I looked at when I testified in court… the face of the man…

Who shot Tina.

I felt my blood beginning to boil; I felt the anger welling inside me. I tried to hear the words of Father John in my head…

"Jack – it's time for you to heal"

For the first time since that day – I was less than a hundred feet from the man who tried to take my life. I was so close to the man who took the life of the little girl I loved so dearly.

What do I do? How was I supposed to feel? At that moment I had to reach deep inside – I had to be the Sheepdog – I had to be the protector… I knew he was no longer a threat to my body, and that he was no longer a threat to my partner… all I knew was I had to protect myself from the feelings – the anger… I had to protect myself from whatever control he thought he had over me.

What did I do? I stood there holding Athena – remembering Tina. We stood together holding the line – the line that I knew I had to protect myself from – the hold he thought he had, but no longer could control. I reached down as if I were going to release Athena from the leash – maybe a way – a way of showing force, but I didn't. My hand lowered, and as I felt her fur – I felt a sense of peace. As if she grounded me in the moment – as if Athena was saving me… from my anger – from my fear.

I stood strong – holding my stare, while I was fighting the anger. Athena stood strong – with a look that could frighten the demons of Hell. She was panting – nearly frothing… and all I could do was to tell her… *"yes little girl… that's the one"* as if she didn't already know.

Two officers finally came to escort him into the building, but before he could reach the doors – he broke from their grip on him, and he turned toward us… and simply motioned with his hand in the makeshift imitation of a pistol, and pretended to 'fire' at us…

Athena let loose with a ferocious growl and bark that made him jump as the housing officers re-secured their grip on him… while all I could do is maintain my constant glare at him…

Athena and I could go home… that poor 'son-of-a-bitch' would spend the rest of his life… walking around in a short circle… of a prison yard.

Eleven minutes. From the time the fence alarms activated to when the prison yard was cleared… eleven minutes. A lifetime of trauma and a moment of clarity… all in eleven minutes. It was those eleven minutes where I realized I could walk away knowing my past no longer held me captive – that this is my life to claim, and my healing to pursue.

I stood strong. Athena was ready, and… I wasn't going to allow myself to succumb to the intimidation of someone who would never again be allowed to walk the streets again freely.

Athena sat on the seat next to me on our drive home. As the truck hummed down the long stretch of highway, the low glow of the setting sun painted the sky in deep oranges and purples, like a bruise healing after the day's battles. Athena rested her head on the center console, her chest still rising and falling with the rhythm of hard-earned calm. She was tired but satisfied, her eyes half-closed, as if even **she** understood the weight of what we'd faced together.

My hands gripped the wheel, not out of tension, but as if anchoring myself to the present. Pride swelled in my chest as I glanced at my partner -

my companion - who had proven once again why she was considered the best. But beneath that pride was something quieter, something deeper. A whisper of Tina's laughter echoed in my mind, her memory as vivid as the streaks of light on the horizon.

I thought about the fragility of life, how easily it could be shattered, and how, even in the pieces, I found strength. Athena had stood beside me today, unwavering, and in *her* steadfastness, I saw a reflection of the protector I once was - the protector I was still trying to be.

As we drove on, the past and the present seemed to merge, not in conflict, but in a quiet understanding. The road stretched ahead, and I let myself feel it all - pride, sorrow, healing, and…

Hope.

Chapter 16

A Ray of sunshine

Athena sat at my feet while I drank my morning coffee. The little patio table offered her the right amount of shade from the sunlight - a shadow of solace from the crisp embrace of autumn's first light. Her ears twitched at the faint sounds of children chattering while walking to school, and I could tell she was relaxed but ever alert, as always.

I stared into the swirls of my coffee, the steam curling up like a lazy ghost – nearly dancing with the smoke from my cigarette. The quiet moments had become something I cherished more than I'd expected. They weren't common in my life – at least not before Athena, not even now. I thought about the training session we had just wrapped up the day before, her precise movements, her unyielding focus. She was a marvel.

But as I sipped my coffee, there was a nagging feeling I couldn't quite shake. Life had a way of throwing shadows across the sunlight. Maybe it was the quiet that made me restless. Or maybe it was just the sense that calm never stayed for long. Bell had already left for a long shift at the hospital, and the quiet of the morning left me wondering… thinking… "It seems like there's always something more."

The ring of my phone broke the stillness. Athena's head snapped up, ears perked, her eyes locking on me as if she knew. I reached for the phone, already bracing myself for the disruption.

"Jack? It's Wade!"

The voice on the other end was familiar -Wade Callahan, my old Army buddy turned Deputy with the Sheriff's department. His tone was tight, urgent, and I hadn't heard from him in quite some time - I knew this wasn't a social call.

"We've got a situation out here. Could use a hand!"

"My grandson is missing – we can't find him anywhere!" Wade nearly shouting! "We've searched everywhere!" Wade's voice cracked, panic bleeding through every word. Athena's ears twitched again, her muscles coiling as if she understood Wade's desperation.

I asked him where he was – and where we could meet. "**I need Gunner**" – "I need you to find my grandson!" I felt a pang at the mention of Gunner. It had been years since my old partner passed, but there was no time for grief now. Wade needed me - and Athena. Wade rattled off the address, his words rushed and uneven. I scribbled it down, my mind already racing through the possibilities. Athena watched me intently, her amber eyes reflecting my urgency. "*Let's go*," I said, grabbing my keys. There was no time to waste. I knew that Wade was aware Gunner had passed away years prior, but I also knew what he meant. He was in a state of panic, and I wasn't about to correct him at a time like this. Athena was alert as if she could tell - she was ready to help.

I told Wade Athena and I were on our way. We left so quickly that I hadn't put Athena's 'gear' on her. Like Tina – she seemed to have that instinct – that natural ability to know something's up.

We started driving and I called Isabel. "We're on our way to help Wade. He's lost his grandson and needs our help." I told her I wasn't sure how long we'd be and that I'd keep her updated. I called Wade back – instructing him to remain calm, and to have his daughter and son-in-law gather some unwashed clothing for Athena.

Athena and I pulled up to Wade's daughter's house, and there were already some of Wade's Sheriff's friends vehicles parked outside. Athena nearly knocked me over as she jumped from the truck, she could sense the excitement. I called her back to me, and we were greeted by Wade – his face pale - washed with fear as he grabbed my arm, his hands shaking - as if he was holding on to dear life.

I could see through the front room window Wade's wife and daughter pacing – the other Deputies trying to comfort them. I knew by now that Wade's Deputy Partners had already asked where the toddler was last seen, but out of habit I asked Wade anyway.

"They - they said he was playing in the back yard, and when my daughter went out to call him for a morning nap – she couldn't find him!" Wade's voice cracking with stress…

I assured him we were going to do everything we could – "We'll find him Wade – trust me" as I did my best to hide my own fear of knowing the possibilities, the many things that could happen.

Athena walked close by my side as we walked into the front room of the house. The child's mom and grandmother's faces were red and their eyes moist – while Wade's son-in-law sat on the couch holding his head in his hands – bent down to his knees. I told Wade to sit down as I began to question again to see if there was anywhere the child could have gone.

One of Wade's officers handed me a small bag of clothing "This is from last night," he said, his voice cracking. Athena sniffed the fabric, her body tensing. Her sharp, searching eyes flicked to me as if to say, "*I've got this*." I placed a hand on her head briefly, grounding myself in her calm confidence. "*Let's find him*," I said, and then… she sat. Athena simply sat for a moment as if she had found him, and then she raised her head – nose twitching, her head pointing toward a nearby hallway.

It might not have been the best thing for me to say, but I had to ask – "you all searched the house didn't you?" Frustrated by my question - they all said they looked everywhere…

Wade just looked at Athena with disappointment – the Deputies were puzzled and Athena… she slowly stood, her eyes scanning and carefully stepped toward the hallway. I looked at the group, but was focusing on Wade, and by now I could tell his confidence in Athena was failing fast. I started to follow Athena toward the hallway.

Wade stood back up – it looked like he was about to say something, but I stopped him before he could speak. "Wade – you have to trust me – you have to trust Athena."

I turned again toward my partner as she led me down the hall. I couldn't help but wonder if a family member… then I thought again – "No - not Wade's family" as my suspicious mind tried to wipe away a lifetime of darkness. "Please God – let's find him safe…"

Athena passed by a couple of open doors to vacant bedrooms, and then sniffed at the door to the master bedroom. Not far behind us was the curious group obviously wondering what my 'girl' was going to do. I asked if it was 'ok' to open the door, and Wade said "yes."

I unlatched the handle and slowly opened the door. Athena sprang up onto the king-sized bed – disheveled and unmade, and she started to nose at the blankets that appeared to have been tossed between the wall and the nearby bed. She 'indicated' she found something by sitting – pointing her nose toward the space between the wall and the bed – and then she let out a bark.

"Wade?" I said with a question… with Athena now digging at the blankets – "did anyone look behind here?"

Wade's daughter sprang up alongside Athena and helped her pull the blankets away from the wall. Athena let out another bark – a smile beaming from her face.

There napping peacefully was the little rascal – who decided to take a nap on his parent's bed, and probably rolled off wrapped in the blankets during his slumber. The mood in the house was turned to elation – smiles now replaced the stress, and Athena was hugged and loved. The boy's mom sobbed with relief, Wade exhaled – near exhausted… but smiled tearfully as his fears were calmed.

Knowing the trauma Wade has from his years diffusing and disarming explosives – bombs – *that* alone can tear at someone's nerves. But compounded with his life in Law Enforcement, and the thought of losing his grandchild . . . ? I gently escorted him away so we could have a quiet moment on the front porch. Wade shifted uncomfortably on the porch step, avoiding my eyes. Athena rested her head on his knee, her quiet presence offering the kind of comfort words couldn't. He stroked her fur without thought, his rough hands trembling less with each pass.

"I'm sorry you had to see me like this, Jack," he said after a long silence, his voice raw and uneven. "It's not like me to… to cry."

I lit a cigarette, taking a slow drag before responding. "Forget what you've always been told, Wade," I said, my voice calm but firm. "Forget the notions of what the world expects of us. We're human. We're allowed to feel."

He glanced at me, the vulnerability in his eyes barely masked by his pride.

I leaned back against the porch railing, looking out at the street where the Sheriff's cars had just left. "You know what Father John used to tell me?" I asked, my voice softening. "He'd say, 'You can't carry the weight of the world if you're not willing to share your own.'"

Wade's grip on Athena tightened briefly, and then relaxed. "I don't know how to… let it out," he admitted, his gaze fixed on the horizon.

I turned to face him, my tone gentle but insistent. "You just did. It's okay to cry, Wade. It's okay to feel scared, overwhelmed - even broken. It doesn't make you weak. Hell, it makes you human. And it's what makes us stronger in the end."

In that moment I felt the guilt – this time, for how often I'd hid my own emotion. Sure – when I was with father John, or alone, I could, but now… I felt like a hypocrite. But I continued…

"You can't always control emotion – and letting it build, well Wade – letting it build up – can kill us! We don't hide laughter; we let it out – because that's what we've been taught. Wade, you can't let what the world expects – you can't let it control you."

His shoulders sagged, the tension slowly ebbing away. He let out a shaky breath, and for a moment, we just sat there, the quiet of the porch broken only by the distant laughter from inside the house.

"Today wasn't easy," I said after a while. "It was a trigger - brought back memories you've been trying to bury. But burying them doesn't make them go away. It just makes the weight heavier."

Wade nodded, his jaw clenching as tears welled in his eyes again. "I've been fighting this for so long," he whispered.

"And you don't have to do it alone," I said, placing a hand on his shoulder. "Come to our meetings. Share your story, your struggles. It's not weakness, Wade - its survival. And it's a hell of a lot easier when you've got people who understand."

He exhaled deeply, wiping his face with the back of his hand. "I'll think about it," he murmured, his voice steadier now.

Athena nuzzled him again, her tail wagging softly, as if to say she was proud of him too.

We sat there for a while longer, the weight of the day slowly lifting as we talked. For the first time in years, I saw a flicker of hope in Wade's eyes - a glimmer of the man he used to be and the strength he still carried within.

Time wasn't important - not now. This moment wasn't about anything other than being present, about being the friend Wade needed. I made a quick call to Bell to let her know I'd be a little longer, but beyond that, nothing else mattered.

As the evening deepened, the porch became a quiet sanctuary, the kind of place where words weren't always necessary, where the simple act of sitting side by side was enough. Wade's breathing slowed, his shoulders loosening as if he were finally letting go of a weight he hadn't realized he was carrying.

"I don't know how to thank you," he said softly, his voice still rough but steadier now.

I shook my head. "You don't need to. That's what friends do, Wade. We show up."

The storm clouds on the horizon crept closer, their dark edges brushing against the fading orange sky. But even as the sun dipped lower, it made one last, defiant attempt to break through. A single ray of light pierced the clouds, casting a warm, golden glow over the porch.

Wade noticed it too, his lips curling into a faint, almost reluctant smile. "Guess that's a sign, huh?"

"Could be," I said, leaning back against the railing. "Maybe it's telling us there's always light, even in the darkest places. We just have to look for it."

He nodded, his hand resting on Athena's head as she leaned into him. And for the first time, I felt it too - the beginnings of healing he hadn't realized... and a real feeling like *my* healing...

Was truly possible.

Chapter 17

They Called Me "Preacher"

Although it felt good - the long day with Wade was exhausting. I truly believe emotional exertion is much harder than physical.

Athena and I hadn't eaten all day. I knew she was hungry. I knew I was. We drove to our little burger place, and as if they knew by the sight of our truck – we would want our usual.

The sunlight had faded into the darkening clouds, behind the horizon, and now it was the glow of the streetlamps in the parking lot that cast its light on our evening meal.

The night shadow of the growing clouds was nothing unusual for the beginnings of a Rocky Mountain autumn. In the distance we could see the flickering of light nature shared. We could hear the faint rumblings of thunder… I told Athena *"see – I was hungry."* She let out a huff – as if she could really laugh.

We ate in silence, listening to the natural world around us. There was a strange kind of peace in it - the kind that comes just before something breaks. I could feel it building. The storm on the horizon was no longer distant; it was drawing closer, and nature was about to unleash its fury.

As we finished our meal, the flashes of lightning were now brighter, the thunder louder and more insistent. My phone buzzed on the seat next to me, pulling me out of my thoughts. It was Bell.

"Jack, the power just went out - and the generator at the hospital isn't kicking on," she said, her voice edged with worry. "The ER's gone dark except for the battery backups on critical systems. None of us knows how to start it... we called maintenance, but he's over an hour out." She paused with a sigh in her breath, then added, "I figured you'd know what to do."

I looked out toward the storm clouds looming over the city, their ominous swell matching the weight in my chest.

"I'm on my way," I told her, already grabbing my keys. I tossed the last of my fries to Athena. She caught them mid-air, tail wagging - still unaware of the chaos brewing.

We hit the road, the headlights cutting through the early darkness as the first heavy drops of rain began to splatter against the windshield. Athena, ever alert, shifted her focus to the storm outside, her ears twitching at each crack of thunder.

By the time we reached the hospital, the storm was in full swing. Bell met me at the side entrance, her face illuminated by the dim emergency lights. "It's worse than I thought," she said, her voice steady but edged with worry. "Half the systems are offline, and the rest won't hold for long."

Athena stayed by my side as we worked. Her presence was a quiet reassurance in the chaotic moments that followed. By the time the generator roared to life, I could feel the tension easing, though the night was far from over.

My radio began to chatter with calls – all over the city, neighborhoods; entire sections of the area were losing power. The lightning triggered power substations all over the valley to shutdown. Dispatch was calling for any – for *all* available officers to respond to the growing darkness all around.

I kissed Bell – she 'wished me luck' as Athena and I ran through the intense rain. I closed the door to the truck and felt a brief moment of being dry as Athena shook her coat and scattered drops all through the truck. I could smell that familiar smell of wet fur, and it too was a comfort knowing she was by my side.

For a moment my thoughts were to drive to my house and retrieve my foul weather gear – heavy rain-coat and hat that could help in a moment like this, but as we pulled out of the hospital parking lot – the rain began to 'let-up' – but the lightning didn't.

The storm had worsened. The flashing of lightning, so intense it painted the entire valley in white-blue hues, had now become a constant barrage. The clouds rolled in thicker, a churning mass of gray-black fury. I told dispatch 'we' were back 'in-service' – then we were told to report to a shopping center immediately. "Multiple reports of looting in progress. All available units, respond."

I let out a low growl under my breath, knowing this was the kind of situation no one wanted to handle - especially not in this weather. Athena's ears perked up as the urgency in my voice sunk into her senses. Her paws shifted uneasily on the truck's seat, but I knew she was ready.

As I pressed the accelerator, the truck surged forward into the storm once again. The shopping center was only minutes away, but with the grid down and streets flooded; I knew it would take longer. I activated my overhead emergency lights and could see people standing in the storm – confused, curious, yet cautious. The flashing of my lights seemed to dance with each burst of lightning.

The thought of what we might find there - people desperate in the face of a storm and a city in darkness - sent a chill down my spine.

The storm had a way of amplifying things, turning the simplest sound into an ominous threat. I tried to push aside the unease, focusing instead on Bell, and what I might be walking into once we reached the shopping center. She'd be fine - I knew she would be - but that didn't stop my worry. Streetlights were out, leaving long stretches of blackness between the occasional flash of lightning. I pulled into the shopping area parking, and the scene in front of me made my heart skip a beat.

There were figures moving in the shadows - dark silhouettes dashing between storefronts, the sound of breaking glass slicing through the booming thunder. My hand instinctively went to the pistol holstered at my side, though I wasn't sure how much good it would do against the chaos unfolding before me.

"Athena, stay close girl," I muttered, my voice thick with resolve.

She gave me a low growl, her alert eyes scanning the scene as we parked the truck a little off the main street, out of sight for the moment. We'd need to move quietly - discretion was our best option here.

I grabbed the radio, reporting in again that we were on scene. I Requested backup for looting. I didn't know if the many suspects could have been "armed and dangerous."

I could hear the commotion grow louder in the background as more officers responded, but I knew help wouldn't get here fast enough.

Athena's low growl rumbled again as we began moving toward the first storefront. My senses were heightened, every crack of thunder feeling like an announcement of the chaos that would follow.

This wasn't just another storm. This was a test of patience, of resolve, and of survival. And it wasn't over yet.

As more officers converged on the shopping center I started directing the growing team to cover as many of the entrances and storefront windows as they could. There was the sound of even more law enforcement units from all over rolling in. It filled the air with a comfort only a Cop could understand. Deputies from the Sheriff's department were joining in to help, adding to our growing presence.

Stan and Aries said they'd cover the other side of the complex, and I told Wade to come with me – as the crowd of looters began to flee from all the 'cops' showing up.

We were clearing one of the stores when I caught a glimpse of Wade's hand twitching. It was subtle - he tried to hide it, but I knew the signs.

Not a lot of us could do this job without carrying something heavy in our hearts. We all had our ghosts.

Wade stood at the end of an aisle; scanning the darkness where only the faintest light from a dying flashlight flickered. His voice broke the silence. "Yeah, tomorrow this'll all be a bad memory, right?"

I raised an eyebrow as I glanced over at him. "Kinda like 'crisis + time = humor?'" I couldn't help but smirk, trying to lighten the mood.

He chuckled weakly, but his smile didn't quite reach his eyes. It was a small thing, but it was a step.

I moved closer, checking the store's back room, making sure he was still with me. Not that I expected him to break, but after everything we'd talked about earlier, I wasn't about to leave him hanging. His progress didn't need a spotlight, but it deserved recognition.

I'd seen too many men - too many of us - forget that just because we couldn't see the scars on the inside didn't mean they weren't there. But scars and all – we kept going. Our presence kept the property safe, and a number of arrests were made. We had a number of the Officers set a perimeter at the shopping center - before Athena and I were off again to help elsewhere.

The storm had passed quickly. One minute the rain came down like a wall, relentless and pounding. The next, it had stopped, as if nature had decided it was done. But the damage was already done. Lightning had taken out the power grid, sending it into a blackout that felt unnatural.

The city felt like it had been erased. All the streetlights were down, leaving behind a void of pitch-black silence, broken only by the occasional flash of light in the distance from a still-flickering transformer or the low hum of radio calls.

It wasn't the rain that would keep us busy - it was the damage from the lightning. The City had taken a beating, and the repairs would take hours.

Athena stayed close, always by my side, keeping me grounded as we drove through the darkened streets, scanning for anything out of place. The flickering of lights on the horizon seemed to mock us, reminding us that everything was still broken.

The hours stretched on. We cleared more stores, kept the peace, and watched the city sleep in its chaos. By the time the storm had completely blown over, the power grid was still down. But there was something about the quiet after a storm - it was an eerie calm since the system wasn't fully restored. The world around us was still dark, but there was a softening in the air, a sense that the worst was behind us. I checked in with dispatch once more. They said repairs would take time, but we had it under control.

The next morning, the sky was clearer. Not completely bright, but at least the sun was making an effort to peek through. The damage from the storm would take longer to fix, but the most pressing concern was keeping order, and we did. I soon found myself outside the church after that long, restless night, seeking Father John's guidance as the city began to stir again.

**

"It was quite a night – huh Jack?" Father John said with a tired grin – probably from the lack of sleep from the storm… "It sure was Father – for all of us."

We 'chatted' for a few minutes – about the storm, and about Wade. I told him that I invited my friend to the meetings, and that he might benefit from "visits with Father John."

Father John smiled… and I continued:

"It felt good to help someone – like I'd helped – not by sharing my story, but really getting close to someone who needed it. I was surprised at what I was saying, but it felt good."

Father John leaned in with encouragement "And that's something worth sharing Jack. It's not only your *story* that could inspire others in '*our*' community, but the insight you've gained over these past few years. Jack, what you have inside needs to be shared!"

I sat in silence within a myriad of thoughts – the emotions, the pain… yes – still there. But I now felt more in control this morning… more so than I have for a very long time. Then Father John gave me that smile – that dangerous smile that told me something else was coming…

"Jack - I'd like to invite you to speak at church this Sunday. What do you think?"

"Really Father, again?" I said with a smirk. "Well - I'll think about it - when can I get back with you?"

Father John went on: "I'd like to know soon Jack, you have a unique perspective, and your experiences could resonate with many who are facing their own struggles. You don't have to have all the answers - I just want you to speak from your heart."

"I guess I could try. I just hope I don't trip over my words, or say something stupid... I'll let you know soon"

Father John grinned warmly "Just remember, you're not alone. We're all here to support you."

I went to turn away for a moment, but stopped... "Father - you know what I was always told from a young age – about strong men not showing emotion – well... thank you... these past few years have taught me I can do, what I was told I couldn't... you've really helped me..."

Father John stood stoic, and somber, he looked deep into my eyes. He said: "you know Jack,

Tina - may have saved you, in more ways than one."

His words hit me, as if hit by a train… as I thought about it, I thought again and again… it's true. If it weren't for losing Tina, I may never have been able to understand the sorrow that allowed me to feel the pain I didn't know I was hiding, and a way to find my way out of the darkness, and be able to walk into the light.

**

I hadn't called Father John back yet. Truthfully, I was still mulling over how I could find the words - or even the courage - to stand up there and share my story again... And I was in no rush to make a decision.

A few days later, Bell and I sat at the diner with our usual crowd of cop and biker friends, each of them cradling a cup of coffee. The morning hum was alive with chatter, and I was beginning to relax, enjoying the comfortable, familiar rhythm of the place. I had my back turned from the doorway, and didn't see him coming. I was surprised to see Father John walk up to our table. I glanced up, only to realize the good Father was looking straight at me, wearing that grin (again) that spelled trouble.

"Jack," Father John announced loudly enough for the whole café to hear, "I'm so glad you've decided to speak at church this Sunday!"

The whole Diner went quiet, and then erupted into laughs and whistles.

"Oh, is that so, **Preacher**?" one of my friends jeered, giving me a good-natured shove. Another one chimed in, "Well, we wouldn't miss this for the world!"

I gave Father John a long look, one that could only mean, *"You're going to pay for this."*

But the good Father just smiled knowingly as he sat with us to have coffee. And somewhere beneath my reluctant grin, there was a spark of warmth. It seemed like the right thing to do - even if I wasn't ready to admit it yet.

**

The following Sunday, my wife and granddaughter walked me into the church, and Bell made sure I was sitting on the front row. I wanted to sit in the back - just in case I needed to make a 'hasty' retreat... I really didn't want to do this.

I can't say why I was so afraid to speak, I sat quietly thinking, and then my thoughts were interrupted by Father John calling my name...

I took a steadying breath as I stepped up to the podium; Father John gave me a gentle pat on the back as he started to step away. He made a final nod with his head while looking toward the stand, and smiled. I stood scanning the familiar faces in the congregation. Neighbors. Friends. My community. They were the people I'd spent my life protecting, and now they looked at me with an expectation that made my hands feel a little heavier.

I gripped the edges of the pulpit, fumbling at first, feeling the weight of my own story. "I... uh..." I cleared my throat, stammering a bit before looking out again. "A few nights ago, I had a dream."

The room was quiet, the kind of quiet where you know every word matters.

"In the dream, I was standing by a river, facing a choice: to cross at the rushing torrent - where the current was fierce and I might not make it - or to search for an easier path. I felt the pull to step into that raging water, though I knew it wouldn't be easy. I could feel the danger. But I also knew…I wouldn't be crossing it alone."

I paused, scanning the faces in the crowd again, feeling the support in their eyes, though I wasn't completely certain that I could go on, but I did…

"You see, at that river, I had to ask myself two questions – two questions I think I heard from a movie: *'Had I found joy in my life?'* And *'Had I brought joy to others?'* I looked back at the years - the darkness I'd lived through, the tough decisions, the friends and family who had stood by me - and finally, I could answer the first question with a 'Yes.' Only now, after all this time, I can say that I have found joy."

A soft murmur rippled through the crowd. I nodded, steadying myself again.

"But that second question…" I let the words linger. "That question…'*Have I brought joy to others?'* That's one I'm still working on, friends.

"I have looked the devil in the face. I have walked through the fires of hell. And through all that, I've tried to bring a little safety, a little comfort, and a little peace. I don't know if that's joy, but I hope it's enough to make a difference."

I paused again, letting the honesty settle between us. The silence gave room for a deeper truth I hadn't always acknowledged.

"But I know this - I couldn't have survived by walking alone. I had my wife, Father John..." I nodded toward him, and then looked over at Izzy and Bell. "I had friends and loyal partners who stood beside me, men and women who served selflessly. I lost a partner, my Tina, who sacrificed without hesitation, without any thought for herself, and that, my friends, is what love truly is."

Heads nodded; I felt their understanding in that shared silence. And so, I kept going.

"Love," I continued, feeling the weight of the word. "The very essence of love is that willingness to serve others – to sacrifice for others - without thinking of ourselves. And I've had the privilege of serving with people, and even my K9 partners - who have done just that. That's a gift - a calling, and it's what's kept me going through my darkest days."

I finally looked down at the polished wooden surface of the podium. The grain caught the light, but my focus shifted to what rested there. Father John's Bible lay open, its well-worn pages gently curled, the passage highlighted as though waiting for this moment. John chapter 15 verse 13:

"Greater love hath no man than this, that a man lay down his life for his friends."

I paused; I took a breath, and then read the passage out loud. It was hard for me to utter the words, but said "true selfless sacrifice – true love, whether it is human, or even if it comes from a dog! It doesn't matter... it's still true love." I paused, and then caught my breath again... "For so long I hadn't realized that my partner – a dog – truly lived what Father John has been preaching to you all – to serve – to sacrifice – to love..."

For a moment, the room blurred as emotion welled up. But with it came a strange and comforting clarity.

I took another deep breath, feeling it move through me, carrying away the heaviness. Then I let the words flow, confessing what had been locked inside for so long: my journey from anger and blame toward God.

"In those days of blaming God for my loss, of facing down that darkness alone, I thought I'd lost myself. But somewhere along the way, I realized it was my own heart I was wrestling with. I was the one keeping myself from the light. And it's only now that I see this…that my course has been a path from confusion to clarity, from shadow to light."

My gaze swept across the room, landing on familiar faces and strangers alike, and I felt the calm settle over me like a steady hand on my shoulder.

"So I stand here to tell you…I survived. And I survived because of every hand that's helped me, every hand that's lifted me up when I was down, and every person who's stood by my side. If I can leave you with anything, it's this: Be that hand for someone else. Because none of us are ever really walking the path – alone."

After I finished speaking, I began to turn so I could take my seat. "Hold on there a second Jack" Father John pulling my arm and turning me back toward him… "There's a little something more we need to do up here…"

Right as he was saying all this - Izzy had walked toward the back of the audience, and opened the big double doors. The click of the latches seemed to echo through the hall. The doors opened with a hint of a squeak, and I saw Stan, with about a half dozen of my friends from the department, all in uniform.

Stan handed Izzy a large package, probably 18 inches by 24, wrapped in brown paper, and she led this procession up to the stand, where Bell was now standing at my side also… with a huge smile.

I was now surrounded by friends and family - supported by my community… Father John, beaming with pride as he announced: "Jack - you've been through a lot these past few years, and I know you have made great strides in overcoming these challenges… we'd like to present you with a little token of our appreciation… Jack - this will forever be a little symbol that represents your journey - the sacrifices both you and your partners have made…"

I began to tug at the paper - I began to tear at it a little, reluctant at first… maybe even a little embarrassed… but as I unwrapped I began to see… I could hardly breathe at first, and then felt the reassurance of Bell's hand on my shoulder. Father John smiling - Izzy beaming with pride… Stan, and the crew – even Wade, all stood fast, a hint of moisture in their eyes. In that moment, in that fleeting instant… I knew I could accept that my journey - my struggles could now make way for a ray of sunshine to brighten my path.

I now know that I can commit to embrace a future with hope, and honor, and a renewed sense of purpose. I felt a sense of closure from grief - while looking to the future…

There I stood - looking at the familiar sight of me, my police truck - the picture with Tina at my side, and professionally photo-shopped at my other side - was Athena… both of my little girls - as if looking at each other… in the clouds behind us were the fond memories of my partners past – ears perked, and ready to defend me – as if somewhere beyond the rainbow bridge. Centered in the images of my memories – shadowed in the clouds of artistry, was Gunner… my first – but not the last.

I tried to hold back my emotions, but I felt safe being surrounded by those who care about me…

Yes – I finally felt the healing, the release, and the courage. I stood there with the tears in my eyes falling freely, and I didn't care anymore, because… sometimes…

"Big boys can cry."

Chapter 18

The Epilogue

My wife told me that she would meet me a little later, and wished me luck as I went to my group meeting. I walked out the door – still sad, but with a new determination to move forward.

I pulled up to the back of the church building, and before I met the group in the recreation hall, I walked slowly up the stairs to the office. The door creaked open with a familiar greeting, and I walked in.

I stood there for a moment looking – staring at the familiar sites and remembering the many conversations. I walked over to the desk and looked down at the many papers and notes... and the Bible.

I took a seat in the big leather chair, and thumbed through the pages, and found the passage that meant so much to him.

John Chapter 15 verse 13... and next to the highlighted passage was the little 'sticky-note' he'd wrote... "For Jack and Tina. It's hard to forget a dog that has given us so much to remember." I was all by myself, but I didn't feel alone. I could still feel him in the room with me – still coaching me... still comforting me.

I closed the book, and held it to my chest. I sat quiet and looked at a picture he still had poised and proud on his desk. Old and now faded – a picture of two soldiers in a small frame. Scribbled at the bottom of the picture was that same passage that meant so much to him... John 15:13.

It was hard, but I stood – I didn't want to leave, but duty now dictated what I had to do. I placed the little picture atop the Bible before I walked back down the stairs and met the men and women who have relied on him so heavily, and they all stood there waiting to greet me. The banter and jokes were now quiet, a faint shadow of the lively conversations we usually had before our meetings. Now the mood was reflective, tempered by a feeling of loss. Our jeans and jackets now replaced by suits and dresses, and even still – many of us wore the uniforms he had grown to love. Veterans, First responders of all sorts; even dispatchers, doctors and nurses – any and all who witness the tragedies of life now gathered together to honor a man who helped us all through the struggles to remain normal. I poured a cup of coffee, and we all took our seats and took turns remembering our friend, our mentor.

It was me now – leading the group's discussions. It was me now who was relating the story of loss – of trauma, and of fear… it was my turn to share, and it wasn't easy.

Isabel walked in as we were finishing our conversations, and she whispered… "It's time."

We all walked across the hallway and stepped quietly into the chapel – reverent, solemn, and respectful. I choked back my feelings listening to the organist play "Nearer my God to Thee" and took my seat on the stand next to Bell.

Father Brian spoke, and so did some of the family members. And then… Father Brian announced a musical number – Father John's favorite song "In The Shadow of The Cross."

The last stanza of the song struck me – it meant more to me than a thousand sermons I could have listened to:

"In the Shadow of The Cross we find our peace"

"In Jesus' love all burdens cease"

"Through every trial – with every loss"

"We find hope in the Cross"

For the third time I stood in front of the congregation. I placed the book he cherished on the podium, and looked down at the picture of Father John, and his childhood friend – hoping it would give me strength to do what he wanted me to do. It was almost as if I gripped that book – the same way I would grip Tina's leash, hoping I could hold on to him the same way I wanted to hold on to Tina.

"It has been a little more than a year since I stood here – it wasn't easy for me then, and it isn't easy for me now. I don't feel like I lost a friend, a mentor, a counselor – I feel like I gained an Angel in heaven – who could keep an eye out for me like he's coaching me from above."

I could feel my sadness, but then a sense of comfort, and I continued… "He taught me that keeping the good memories would mean I really didn't lose something, but would carry those moments with me always…"

I paused for a moment unsure of how to proceed, but I thought about the lesson he may have wanted me to share… "What Father John taught me was that I wasn't alone. He taught me that I wasn't walking the path of healing without help. He taught me that he truly understood as no other could… and he was right."

I opened his little black leather bound book to the passage and stared at it for a second. "I'd like to share a story that Father John didn't share with very many people…" and I went on.

I told the congregation about the night in Viet Nam Father John lived through – only because his childhood friend kept him alive. "It wasn't just a story - it was a glimpse into the depths of his faith, his struggle, and his humanity. Even now, its weight lingers, like a lesson I will carry with me forever. This story, his story is the message of true love – of an ultimate sacrifice. His friend didn't just save my mentor… but saved me, he saved so many of us too - in many ways."

I looked at the many faces of people that have been helped by my friend, and choked back in my voice and said: "the man that saved Father

John… saved every one of us that have been helped by him." I went on to explain that his story not only shaped the way I saw him, but changed the way I saw myself. "Father John once told me that someday – I too could be the light that would help someone else. I didn't fully realize this until today.

"Until today – I may not have realized that my partner – Tina – by saving me may have been the force that could save others as well."

**

After the service concluded – we all proceeded to the church cemetery where a Military Honor Guard performed the 21 gun salute, and the ceremonial folding of the Flag. His final resting place was next to a man who held our dear Father's life in his hands, and who sacrificed himself so others could come to know the love and service we have come to depend on.

Draped gently across the crafted stone of granite – the monument for 'his' friend, was a colored ribbon and medal now faded from the years of weather – a medal no one could bring themselves to touch… and at the base of the tribute stone was a simple inscription…

"Walk Softly – Resting here is a Hero who will forever hold in his hands… A Piece of My Heart"

**

I've lived a lifetime of facing the things too painful for most, even too painful for me, but I wasn't alone. My wife, my dogs, and Father John – and a growing group for support have given me hope. My journey hasn't been easy, but like Father John said: "Tough times call for strong men" and I can only hope I would never let him down.

Our drive toward home was quiet, but not silent. Both Bell and I remembered the funny moments we'd spent with Father John, and it made us feel like he would have wanted us to remember him that way. He wouldn't have wanted us to remember how frail he'd become – or how his health had diminished recently…

Father John would want us to remember his crooked smile, his wisdom and wit. He would have wanted us to "drive-on" and not be sad. He would have wanted us to have the joy we all deserve.

I could tell by her smile – that Isabel had something on her mind. I looked at her and said "what ya thinking?" She said "a couple of months ago he called on one of the members of the congregation to open the service with prayer. I guess this guy felt honored – and he prayed, and prayed, and prayed and kept going on… when he finished Father John approached the pulpit and said *our next speaker will be…*'" I burst out laughing and said "he really said that?" still chuckling "I guess I could really see him doing that." Bell said "I'll miss his humor…"

Bell and I stopped at our café where we met a large group of our friends. We all reminisced about the man who helped us all. We all agreed that we should drink a toast in his honor, and knew he would want us to laugh.

So we did.

We enjoyed good memories, conversation, laughter, and maybe even a few tears. I sat in the café, nursing my second cup of coffee, and I noticed a young man in a crisp, newly issued police cadet uniform walk through the door. At first, I didn't recognize him, but when he smiled, it clicked.

We shook hands, and he pulled up a chair. "I wanted to thank you. What you said to me that day a few years ago - it stayed with me. Got me through a lot."

He told me about his father's passing and how he'd found a purpose in the loss. "You and Father John… you both showed me what it means to be strong. I figured, maybe I could try to do the same for someone else someday."

I looked at him, trying to think of something profound to say, but all I could do was grin. "You're gonna do just fine, kid. Just don't forget - being strong doesn't mean you're invincible. It means you keep going, even when it's hard."

I had no idea at the time I went on a Sunday ride – feeling the grief, the loss, and the anger – that a young man facing his own struggles would find anything of value in those few words I said.

**

When Bell and I got home we were greeted by the familiar wet nose and cheerful eyes. I smiled and walked to the picture I was given a little more than a year ago… I stood there with Athena at my side and touched the image hanging on my wall…

Of my little girl who saved me.

For the first time… I could look deep into her eyes and not think of just the pain, but the sacrifice – the love, and the hope of a bright future she has given me. I stood for a moment with Bell looking on, and I smiled then whispered…

"I Love You Tina."